DOC SAVAGE'S AMAZING CREW

William Harper Littlejohn, the bespectacled scientist who was the world's greatest living expert on geology and archaeology.

Colonel John Renwick, "Renny," his favorite sport was pounding his massive fists through heavy, paneled doors.

Lieutenant Colonel Andrew Blodgett Mayfair, "Monk," only a few inches over five feet tall, and yet over 260 pounds. His brutish exterior concealed the mind of a great scientist.

Major Thomas J. Roberts, "Long Tom," was the physical weakling of the crowd, but a genius at electricity.

Brigadier General Theodore Marley Brooks, slender and waspy, he was never without his ominous, black sword cane.

WITH THEIR LEADER, THEY WOULD GO
ANYWHERE, FIGHT ANYONE, DARE EVERYTHING—
SEEKING EXCITEMENT AND PERILOUS ADVENTURE!

DEVIL
ON THE MOON

A DOC SAVAGE ADVENTURE
BY KENNETH ROBESON

A NATIONAL GENERAL COMPANY

DEVIL ON THE MOON
*A Bantam Book / published by arrangement with
The Condé Nast Publications Inc.*

PRINTING HISTORY
Originally published in DOC SAVAGE *Magazine March 1938*
Bantam edition published July 1970

*Bantam Books are published by Bantam Books, Inc., a National
General company. Its trade-mark, consisting of the words "Bantam
Books" and the portrayal of a bantam, is registered in the United
States Patent Office and in other countries. Marca Registrada.
Bantam Books, Inc., 666 Fifth Avenue, New York, N.Y. 10019.*

PRINTED IN THE UNITED STATES OF AMERICA

CONTENTS

DEVIL ON THE MOON

Chapter I

MAN IN THE METEOR

A roaring sound was probably the first evidence of what was to come to be known as the mystery of the Devil on the Moon. A sick red light accompanied the roaring. It lighted up the surroundings, and struck the earth near the Spanish Plantation.

The Spanish Plantation was situated in Virginia, near Washington, and its old Colonial architecture was pleasantly distinguished. There was a colored orchestra and a sign which advertised chicken dinners. It was a nice place.

Lin Pretti was one among a number who heard the roar. She happened to be standing in a secluded spot on the Spanish Plantation lawn.

Lin Pretti had become something of a sensation around the Spanish Plantation. She was not an exquisitely beautiful girl, but her manners were perfect and her conversation excitingly clever. She grew on people, men especially. Lin Pretti was somewhat mysterious; no one really knew much about her.

Lin Pretti stared at the night sky.

The red, roaring thing came all the way down and dropped out of sight behind a nearby hill. There was a distinct report and an earth jar. Then came silence and darkness.

The falling object that came arching down out of the heavens might have been a meteor, except that meteors or shooting stars usually fade out after a shower of bright, dazzling sparks. They are burned away by friction with the earth's atmosphere.

1

Lin Pretti reacted strangely. Her hands covered her eyes. A terrified sound escaped her. It was as though she knew the real nature of what had happened.

Bob Thomas found Lin Pretti with her hands over her eyes.

"Bo-o-o!" Bob Thomas exclaimed playfully.

Bob Thomas, tall, blond, and rather good-looking, was a young Washington insurance salesman. He admitted being in love with Lin Pretti.

The girl did not seem to hear the "Bo-o-o!"

"Is something wrong?" Bob Thomas asked anxiously.

Lin Pretti suddenly jerked her hands from her face and seized Bob's arm. Her fingers seemed to bite him. The girl swallowed twice before she managed to say, "Nothing." She seemed frantic to get Bob Thomas talking about something besides the way she looked. "Bob," she said quickly, "what —what did you learn of the man I asked you to look up information about?"

"You mean Doc Savage?"

"Yes."

Bob Thomas was impatient. "This Doc Savage is a man who devotes his life to going about the world righting wrongs and punishing evildoers. It sounded kind of queer to me." The young insurance man took both the girl's hands in his. "Lin! What is wrong with you?"

"Bob," she exclaimed wildly, "will you help me?"

"Help you do what?"

"Get a flashlight, and be prepared for something so horrible and incredible that you'll have trouble believing it."

Brush grew on the hill behind the Spanish Plantation. Bob Thomas waved the beam of the flashlight he had taken out of his car, picking out the best route. When they topped the hill, Bob Thomas gave a surprised start.

A few hundred yards ahead was water. It was an arm of Chesapeake Bay. Thomas hadn't known the bay was that close.

Lin Pretti raced forward.

"Quick!" the girl gasped.

Bob Thomas followed her until they neared the lake. Then the girl stopped abruptly. She faced Bob Thomas.

"Will you promise me something?" she demanded.

Bob Thomas did not hesitate. "I promise!" he said.

"Don't ever tell anyone what happens tonight!" the girl requested earnestly.

"I promise," Bob Thomas said. He was astounded.

Lin Pretti stared about in the darkness. "It must have struck around here!" she said tensely.

This puzzled Bob Thomas; he'd been inside the Spanish Plantation, had not seen the strange, roaring red thing come out of the night sky. The girl reached for the flashlight. He let her have it. She ran forward, searching.

"Look here!" Bob said. "If there is anything dangerous around, it's no place for a girl. Maybe I'd better take you back!"

The girl just shuddered.

Bob Thomas obeyed a natural masculine impulse and put his arm around the young woman.

Lin Pretti looked up at him. "Bob—you love me, don't you?" she said.

"By George, if I don't, I'll do until the next guy comes along!" he said heartily.

"Don't, please," the girl said strangely, "because you're too nice a young man to die."

They found the green man lying behind a bush.

He was alive. He had a lot of bony framework; once he must have been a giant. But now there was only hide and gristle on his bones.

The man was not really green. His garment was a cloth like silk, a green hue a little darker than grass. It resembled a suit of tights.

Circling the green man's midriff was a shiny metal belt. Around his neck was a bright metal collar equipped with wing nuts, as if a helmet fitted there.

The green man had been burned badly, and one arm was broken. Probably he had other injuries. He looked at Lin Pretti. Scarlet crept from the corners of his mouth. Suddenly he recognized the girl.

"It has been a long time!" he gasped in accented English.

"Tony Vesterate!" the girl cried.

"Yes." The green man's voice was weak.

"You disappeared two years ago!" The girl bit her lips. "But you look so—so much older."

Agony made the green man's lips peel. "I am thirty-one."

Bob Thomas realized the man looked fifty at least. The fellow seemed to be getting worse.

"I have been on the moon!" he screamed suddenly.

Bob Thomas sniffed skeptically. Then he turned to the girl. But Lin Pretti was stark rigidity from head to foot.

The green man stirred weakly, moaned.

"Have you got a knife?" he croaked.

"Knife?" Lin Pretti looked puzzled. "No."

The green man's hollow eyes sought Bob Thomas. "Have you?"

"Er—not much of a one," Bob Thomas said, showing his knife, a tiny thing on the end of his watch chain.

"Give it to me!" the green man ordered.

Curious to see what the fellow wanted with the knife, Bob Thomas unhooked the tiny blade. He opened it for the man.

The green man twisted, got at his left leg, inserted the blade, and opened the green cloth. The ridge of a healed wound was revealed.

"If you're squeamish, you had better turn around," he said to the girl.

Lin Pretti quickly faced the other way.

The green man had courage. A moment later his shaking fingers were wiping the object he had excavated.

The object was a dark-blue, glasslike cylinder less than half an inch in diameter and no more than two inches long. The glasslike substance was too blue to reveal what was inside.

"Here is what—we were after," the green man said.

Lin Pretti took the cylinder.

"I understand," she said queerly.

The green man pointed toward the inlet. "Go down there and look," he ordered. "It will be interesting."

"We'd better do it, Bob," Lin Pretti said quietly.

Bob Thomas reached reluctantly for the flashlight, and they ran toward the inlet. Bob kept roving the flashlight beam. The bushes were small and thick. When they finally stood on the shore of the inlet, its glassy surface seemed to mock them. Reflection of clouds and stars created an eerie mural on the surface of the water.

There was nothing to be found. They did a good job of searching.

"Queer he'd ask us to come down here," Bob Thomas muttered.

When they went back to where they had left the green man, he was gone.

Chapter II

STRANGE MEN AND STRANGE QUESTIONS

Unexpected absence of the green man was such a shock that Bob Thomas extinguished his flashlight. He could not have explained just why, unless it was a feeling of some terror lurking. Now and then a disturbed bird made a fluttering noise in the brush. Cloud images on the bay resembled monsters and seemed to crawl over the tiny light points of the stars.

"He tricked us!" Bob Thomas muttered.

The girl said nothing.

Bob Thomas pointed his flashlight beam at the ground. Faint bloodstains could be distinguished where the green man had lain. "He was hurt too bad to have gone far. We'll hunt him."

"No!" the girl gasped. She took hold of the young man's arm. "Please, Bob—we've got to leave here," she said wildly.

And because he was in love with her, he followed her. They reached the top of the hill and started down toward the Spanish Plantation before he spoke.

"Lin," he said sharply, "what is this all about?"

The girl walked faster. "Please, Bob! You mustn't ask questions!"

Bob Thomas turned the flashlight on Lin Pretti's face. He saw so much fear that it shocked him. He had thought the girl sounded scared; he had not expected such utter terror. Bob Thomas's skin began to feel as if it wanted to crawl. He suddenly knew there was some incredible terror here, something hidden, something he did not see.

6

"That stuff about the moon—" Bob Thomas demanded suddenly. "What did the fellow mean?"

The girl shook her head slowly. "You would not understand, Bob."

"You're in trouble!" Bob Thomas grumbled. "I should have known that much when you asked me to investigate Doc Savage."

The girl stopped.

"Oh, that!" She shook her head. "That had nothing to do with this. I was just—just curious."

"Do you have to lie to me?"

The young woman threw up her chin and seemed about to fling something biting. Instead, she whirled and ran toward the Spanish Plantation. She flounced inside and slammed the door behind her.

Bob Thomas, his expression more puzzled than hurt, started to open the door. Then he reconsidered. His car, a small coupé, was parked in the nearby lot. He got behind the wheel, tore the top off a package of cigarettes and sat and smoked thoughtfully. After about ten minutes, an idea occurred to him, and he seized his flashlight and got out of the car.

He was going to hunt the green man.

Topping the ridge, he was surprised to see a light moving down near the bay, where he had last seen the green man. When he saw who was using the light, Thomas stopped very still.

Lin Pretti! The girl was removing the bloodstains where the green man had been!

Watching her, Bob Thomas was again impressed by her terror. In fact it was catching. Bob Thomas put a finger inside his collar as if it was tight and was choking his Adam's apple, then rubbed his forehead in puzzlement. His brain would not accept such insanities as the dying man in green had revealed to him and Lin Pretti. And as for being on the moon, that too was ridiculous!

Bob Thomas knew Lin Pretti well enough to believe that she did not scare easily. And yet she was utterly frightened. He wondered what he should do. If he accosted her now, she would be angry. And he doubted if she would answer any questions.

Thinking about the girl, Bob Thomas caught himself wondering just exactly who she was. After all, no one seemed to know where she came from. She didn't have a job evidently. As a matter of fact there was a good deal of mystery connected with her. Bob Thomas didn't like it one bit. It smacked too much of trouble. And Bob Thomas was the type of fellow who didn't go hunting for it.

Of course, if Lin Pretti really needed help badly, he'd be only too glad to help. But something told him Lin Pretti wanted anything but that right now. What she wanted most was to be alone. Bob Thomas gritted his teeth and swore.

While Bob Thomas watched, Lin Pretti moved toward the bay with an armload of bloodstained weeds, which she apparently was going to throw into the water.

She had been gone only a moment when hands unexpectedly took hold of Bob Thomas.

There were several pairs of hand. When Thomas fought them, some of the hands became fists and struck back. He went down with men in a fighting pile.

"Blast him!" a voice grated. "He's not as weak as he looked!"

This was the first time Bob Thomas had ever heard himself called weak-looking. He was six feet two, and he had made a football name in college. He kicked, and heard a victim reel away moaning. Bob got an arm loose, struck. Someone fell heavily.

Clouds passing overhead made it dark. Bob Thomas began to feel confident that he was going to escape—or perhaps he might even whip them all!

"Behemoth!" someone screeched.

The tone which answered this call was one Bob Thomas never forgot. It was a great, gusty whisper. An incredibly cavernous whisper.

"Gimme room to take 'im!" said the whisper.

The men released Bob Thomas, and he stumbled to his feet, but not quickly enough to evade a charge. A great body hit him. Thomas struck back with his fist, hit something that felt more like iron than flesh. Then great arms squeezed him. He was suddenly and completely helpless.

"I got 'im!" said the huge whisper.

A flashlight blazed. Bob Thomas twisted to see what nature of monster held him.

Behemoth was a giant with hair on the back of his hands —bright-red hair—and no hair on his head. His face had freckles, his nose flared, and the bulge of his teeth gave his lower face a squarish effect. His shirt gaped at the neck to show red fur. His shirt had two pockets; both were full of cigars, and he was smoking one.

"Hey!" someone exploded. "This ain't Vesterate!"

It was plain they had thought they were seizing the green man.

The captors scowled at Bob Thomas in disgust.

"Here comes Lurgent!" a man said.

Lurgent came up. He was a tall hawk in a brown suit.

"Hi-ya, boss!" said the giant Behemoth.

Lurgent looked at Bob Thomas. "Who's this?"

"That's what we're wonderin'," Behemoth said.

Lurgent came over and poked Bob Thomas with a finger. "What are you doing here?" he demanded. "Who are you?"

Bob Thomas, baffled, did what he thought wise. He avoided the truth.

"I was dancing at that roadhouse over the hill yonder. I had a spat with my girl and took a walk to cool off. What's the idea of your men grabbing me?"

He thought that was a rather good story. It seemed to deceive the men, too.

"I'm sorry," Lurgent told Bob Thomas politely. "You see, we are guards from a nearby insane asylum, and one of the patients has escaped. We're hunting him. My men mistook you for the—ah—nut." Lurgent glared at Behemoth. "What the hell are you holding him for? Turn him loose!"

Bob Thomas was released. He got to his feet. He killed time straightening his clothes.

Bob Thomas thought over what he had just been told, and the strange things that had happened.

He suddenly recalled that Lin Pretti had never told him why she was in this district. Perhaps she had wished to be close to a relative who was confined in an institution! Suppose the relative had escaped? Naturally, the girl would be concerned, and she might try to cover the truth. She might deny, for instance, that the green man was a demented relative. Most people are sensitive about having insanity in the family.

"How was your escaped maniac dressed?" Bob Thomas asked.

Lurgent grinned. "He's a bad case, and we humor him. Let him wear silly-looking green tights. He once saw a motion picture of a man who went to the moon, and now he imagines he's the man on the moon."

"That explains what he said about being on the moon."

"*You saw him?*" Lurgent yelled.

"Yes," Bob admitted sheepishly.

"But you said you hadn't!"

"I know. I said that because I didn't trust you gentlemen."

"We're sorry, buddy."

"Will you gentlemen tell me something?" Bob asked.

Lurgent granted. "Anything we can."

"Is Lin Pretti a relative of this insane man?"

Lurgent nodded. "His sister."

"Thank you," Bob said. "She was with me when we found the nut—the green man."

"I see." Lurgent seemed quite friendly. "What happened then?"

Bob Thomas launched into a description of what had taken place.

"Who has the blue glass cylinder?" questioned Lurgent, after Bob Thomas had finished.

"Lin has it."

"Where does she stay?"

"At a new brick tourist hotel on the road north of here," Bob said.

"It seems," Lurgent said, "that we are going to have to kill you."

Behemoth whispered, "Murder ain't nothin' to go rushin' into!"

Lurgent scowled and addressed his men: "Tie this Thomas fellow."

Bob fought them. But he had waited too long. They got him down—with Behemoth's aid—and contributed belts to fasten his ankles, and handkerchiefs to put in his mouth.

"I guess we won't kill him!" Lurgent growled at Behemoth. "I'm sending you after the girl."

"You want that glass cylinder, too?" Behemoth asked.

"Of course, you fool!"

Behemoth did not seem insulted. He asked in a mild whisper, "What *is* that capsule, anyhow?"

"That," Lurgent said, "is none of your business."

The giant shrugged. "What about the bird in the green suit —that Vesterate?"

"He'll be with the girl, of course," Lurgent said. He made a meaningful gesture at his throat. "But you don't need to bring back the fellow in green, providing you leave him dead enough."

Bob Thomas knew they were wrong about Vesterate. They didn't know how badly Vesterate had been hurt. Far from being with Lin Pretti, the poor fellow had dragged himself away and was dying somewhere near.

"You heard Thomas say where the girl stays," Lurgent growled at Behemoth. "Get her and bring her here."

Behemoth nodded, then walked away.

Suddenly Bob Thomas' face blanched. For Lurgent had drawn a pistol, a single-shot gun with a long barrel and silencer. Lurgent deliberately aimed this weapon at Bob Thomas' head.

"Wait!" Bob Thomas exploded frantically. "Maybe you'd like to know about the Man on the Moon!"

Lurgent started violently. Seizing a flashlight, he blazed it into Bob Thomas' features. "*What did you say?*"

Lurgent waved at his men to withdraw. They did so, leaving Lurgent and Bob Thomas behind. They were not away for long. There was a single shot.

"Come on back!" Lurgent called.

Bob Thomas was sprawled on the ground, head turned to one side. There was a smear of red on his forehead. Lurgent reloaded his single-shot pistol. He said, "Keep your eyes open while I get rid of the body."

He shouldered the body of Bob Thomas and strode toward the water.

Chapter III

BLUE GLASS ROD

The neon sign said:

DIXIE INN

The inn building was new, large, built of brick; a substantial structure, and as homey-looking as an English farmhouse.

Lin Pretti was staying at the Dixie Inn.

Behemoth, when he reached the hotel, proceeded to talk with the doorman. Eventually a five-dollar bill changed hands, as well as a story about Lin Pretti being a married woman whose husband had hired a detective to trail her.

Behemoth's story now had a second installment. In this second part, Behemoth was an honest detective. Lin Pretti had dropped a ten-dollar bill. Behemoth had found it, and he wanted to return it without revealing his identity. Would the doorman take the bill up to the girl? The doorman would.

Behemoth walked to the rear of the hotel and proceeded to accomplish a remarkable feat. The bricks in the wall were of a coarse type, with deep grooves between them. Using an incredible strength in his fingertips, and employing his bare feet —he first removed shoes and socks—Behemoth climbed the wall.

Soon he was clinging outside Lin Pretti's window.

The girl had two suitcases on the bed, was stuffing them with clothing.

Outside the window, Behemoth clung with the apparent ease of a grotesque bat.

12

When there was a knock on her door, the girl started violently. Then she whipped to the writing desk. An inkwell stood there. She drew something from a pocket of her frock and dropped it into the inkwell.

Lin Pretti then went to the door, opened it, and was handed the ten-dollar bill by the doorman.

Behemoth got the window up silently while she was standing half outside in the hall, talking with the doorman in an effort to learn who had given him the bill.

Lin Pretti backed into the room, closed the door and locked it. Then she stood, looking puzzled, and was that way when Behemoth seized her.

The struggle was short, and Behemoth's furry hand over the girl's mouth kept it silent. Convinced finally of the hopelessness of struggling, the young woman quieted. Behemoth removed his hand carefully from her mouth.

"Where's that blue glass jigger?" Behemoth demanded.

"You—you—" Nervousness almost strangled Lin Pretti. "I can't imagine what you are talking about!"

Behemoth shrugged, used a sheet from the hotel bed to bind and gag the young woman. There were two blankets on the bed and he knotted these together, then made one end of the improvised rope fast under the girl's arms.

Leaving her, Behemoth went to the inkwell. He extracted the blue glass cylinder with a pen, then dried it on the blotter, being careful not to stain his fingers.

He spent some moments examining it curiously, then went into the bathroom, searched and found a roll of ordinary adhesive tape, tore off a strip and proceeded to fasten the blue capsule to his body, just below the armpit, a spot where it was not likely to be damaged. After buttoning his shirt, he lowered the girl from the window and followed her.

Behemoth carried the girl over his shoulder, her weight seeming to mean little to him, and trotted into the night. The distance to the Spanish Plantation was not great. Behemoth traversed the entire stretch at an easy run but avoided the roadhouse and crossed over the hill to the lake. There was a quality almost ghostly about the silence with which he skirted the shore of the lake until he encountered Lurgent and the others.

Behemoth looked around. "Where's that young fellow—Bob Thomas?"

Lurgent shrugged; his words demonstrated that he was an excellent liar. "Couple of the boys took him away," he said. "They'll keep him in a safe place and turn him loose after this all blows over."

Behemoth was silent for so long that Lurgent's hand drifted nervously toward his gun pocket. But Behemoth only grunted and lowered the girl.

Lurgent growled, "Did you get the blue thing?"

"She must have hidden it," Behemoth explained blandly. "She wouldn't tell me where it was."

"What about Vesterate?"

"No sign of him."

"I'll talk to the girl," Lurgent growled.

Lurgent seized Lin Pretti's wrist and bent it cruelly, while two men held the girl and a third kept a cap jammed over her mouth so that her sounds of agony would not be too loud.

"Don't think you'll get anything out of her that way," Behemoth remonstrated.

Lurgent turned, seemed on the point of snarling something, then reconsidered. "Maybe you're right. We'll keep her with us a while."

"Sure. Good idea."

"The green man—Vesterate—worries me." Lurgent picked at his teeth with a fingernail. "Look, Behemoth, go back to that hotel and see if Vesterate shows up. Try to find him."

"Where'll I meet you?"

"Join us at that tourist camp."

"Are you taking the girl there?"

"No. That wouldn't be safe. I'll take her to another place."

Nodding as if satisfied, Behemoth ambled off. He made some noise this time, and Lurgent's men heard him progress well up the hill before the sounds he was making were no longer audible.

"We better be skipping with the girl," a man suggested.

Lurgent made a growling sound. "If you think the girl stays alive, you're crazy!"

"Huh?"

"I'm a kind guy at heart," Lurgent said dryly. "I was sparing Behemoth's feelings. We'll tie the girl, then throw her in the inlet—with her ex-boy friend."

The men squirmed uneasily at this callous talk of killing the girl.

"Listen, Lurgent, is that necessary to . . ."

"Her actions proved just what she is. You know the orders, when we get hold of one of her kind."

The other shuddered.

They found a large rock that was misshapen enough to be tied to the girl with no likelihood of slipping free. They lashed it to her ankles, then carried the young woman to the edge of the inlet.

Two of the men, one on each side, held the girl, and Lurgent said, "All together! One, two—swing her!"

The young woman struck the surface feet first. After she disappeared, one very large bubble came up along with other bubbles that were smaller. The men hurried away as if they did not want to see the bubbles.

Chapter IV

BEHEMOTH, QUEER MAN

It was somewhat later in the night—a bit over an hour—and two voices were conversing tensely in the darkness. One was Behemoth.

". . . it might save a great deal of trouble," Behemoth was saying.

"No," said the other speaker. "You're wasting your time."

"You won't tell me what is behind this thing?"

"I won't tell you anything."

Behemoth seemed patient enough. "Who was the green man—Vesterate or whatever his name was?"

Silence replied.

"What did that stuff about the moon mean?"

More silence.

"Where is the green man?" Behemoth asked.

"I told you, you're wasting your time!" insisted the other voice.

"How about telling me what that little blue glass capsule means?"

A shaky sigh was the only response to this query.

"That's gratitude!" Behemoth complained. "Not only do I pull you out of that inlet after Lurgent threw you in, but I work over you half an hour before you revive."

"Thank you!" said Lin Pretti.

Behemoth made a growling noise. "Too bad I gotta keep my hands off Lurgent!"

"Do you?"

"Course! And to clear up some doubts in your mind—

here's why. By getting into Lurgent's gang and pretending to be one of the gang, I hope to learn what's behind this. Suppose you tell me your story."

"What do you want to know?"

"The whole thing. Then I'll give you what I've learned. We'll swap information and maybe have something."

Lin Pretti shuddered. "It's all so horrible—so impossible. Those things—I still can't think they're men—yet they look like men, only their terrible green garments . . ."

"Wait a minute! What the heck kind of talk is this?"

"The first one came over a year ago." The girl seemed to have trouble controlling her voice. "It was first seen—in my country. No one knew what it was. The initial reports were simply of a man-figure dressed in green tights. Then—then . . ."

"I wonder who's kidding who, here," Behemoth muttered.

"First a man was found dead, then a woman," Lin Pretti continued. "Later two more men—it was terrible! They all died the same way—their bodies becoming a deep blue. And doctors could not explain it."

"Um-m-m." Behemoth scratched his head.

The girl coughed. "We finally realized that the green man —if you could call *it* that—was responsible. The police began to hunt. They fired on *it* several times."

Behemoth grunted.

"It was a farm boy who first uncovered the truth," Lin Pretti continued. "He saw the things landing from the sky in strange machines. The farm boy realized they were coming from the moon. Nobody believed him, of course. It seemed impossible. It does seem impossible, doesn't it?"

"Uh-huh," agreed Behemoth.

"We don't know why the man-things are here, nor do we know how to combat them. If we could only get hold of one of them, we might learn something. The government of my country has agents all over the world looking for the thing. I heard that one of them was here in America, lurking near the Spanish Plantation roadhouse, so I came to find it."

"You did, too."

"I was lucky. The thing acted so strangely when I found it —it seemed to know me—gave me a capsule which looked like blue glass."

"You know what I think, young lady?"

"Eh?"

"You're the tallest liar I ever listened to," Behemoth said.

She did not answer.

Behemoth proceeded to bind the girl and gag her. Then he left her lying there, and went directly to the highway which ran past the Spanish Plantation. There was no traffic this late at night. Behemoth used his flashlight, casting the beam over the road as he walked along.

He came upon two rabbits which lay on the road. They were lifeless and might have been run over by a car during the night. Behemoth stopped when he found the rabbits.

Removing a bit of paper and a pencil from a pocket, Behemoth wrote:

> THING DOES NOT MAKE SENSE YET. LOOK
> AROUND FOR MAN WEARING GREEN TIGHTS.
> HE IS PROBABLY NEAR INLET SOMEWHERE.

Behemoth turned back, dropped this note at the roadside near the rabbits, then hurried on.

A few moments later, a shadowy figure appeared and got the note Behemoth had left.

Later in the night—in fact it was almost dawn—the huge Behemoth appeared at the rear of a rather shabby-looking tourist camp in the vicinity. He carried the bound and gagged girl in his arms. His destination was one of the tourist cabins.

Lurgent opened the door. Sight of the girl made him look as startled as an owl. "Where'd you find her?"

"Oh, just around loose," Behemoth explained.

Silence followed that. Then Lurgent relaxed.

"Swell!" he said. "Did you find Vesterate?"

"No."

Lurgent growled. "Then we'd better get back to the inlet and hunt for him."

Lurgent bawled orders. In a few minutes they were headed toward the inlet.

Morning sunlight on the surface of the inlet made it resemble a mirror as Lurgent, Behemoth and the others, having parked their cars on a road near the Spanish Plantation, reached the shore of the lake.

The men looked around carefully, but it was Behemoth who pointed out the tops of taller trees which had been scorched. He indicated the fact that the scorched tops were in a line leading toward the lake.

Now that it was daylight, the surroundings appeared somewhat different than they had during the night. As they sought the green man's trail, Lurgent gave too many orders, as if trying to rebuild any damage which Behemoth might have done to his prestige.

Behemoth finally located the trail of the green man.

"He lay here for a while, and the girl and Bob Thomas talked to him," Behemoth pointed out. "Then the girl and Bob Thomas walked away from him, as if they were searching, then came back. But in the meantime the green man had fled."

"You a clairvoyant?" Lurgent asked Behemoth.

Behemoth then indicated tiny signs—freshly crushed blades of grass, disturbed dust on leaves—which he claimed were as plain as footprints in mud to him.

"Well, where did that green devil go?" Lurgent snarled.

"This way."

Behemoth pointed out dried drops of crimson on some weeds. These bloodstains were plain enough for all to see.

"The green man was wounded," Behemoth explained. A bit later he showed where the man they were trailing had fallen. "Evidently lay here a while. He was probably here while you were off after the girl."

Lurgent scowled.

"Look!" Behemoth exclaimed. He leveled an arm. The others stared. Lurgent whipped out a gun.

"Who's that?" Lurgent exploded.

The cause of this excitement was a group of five men. Three were running toward the road about two hundred yards distant. Two of the men sat in a large sedan.

The three running strangers were distinctive. One was a huge, soberly dressed fellow with tremendous hands; his fists seemed large and out of proportion. The second man was a lean, dapper fellow, remarkably well-dressed, carrying a black sword cane. But the third man was the most unusual of the lot, being short, almost as broad as tall. He resembled an ape dressed in a hand-me-down suit. This fellow was trailed by a pig distinguished by amazingly large ears.

These strangers were carrying the green man toward the car.

Behemoth emitted a howl. Diving a hand into a pocket, he brought out a gun, leveled it, fired.

The trio carrying the green man whirled. They seemed startled. Then they dashed for the car with their burden.

Behemoth emitted another howl and let fly more bullets. "C'mon! You paralyzed?" he snapped at Lurgent.

Lurgent acted as if he were in a trance. He didn't move for a minute. Something seemed to have happened to him; his eyes were wide, his mouth open, his face pale. His knees appeared to be made of rubber. He tried to say something, said, "*Wah-wah-wah*" instead of words. He acted as if he had suddenly been smitten with a powerful disease that had momentarily rendered him powerless to act as he normally would have.

Behemoth, looking disgusted, ran toward the strange trio who had the green man. Behemoth was not fast enough. His quarry got to the car. Behemoth stopped, planted himself on widespread feet, took deliberate aim, and emptied his revolver.

The car departed with no more concern than if Behemoth had been firing blank cartridges.

Behemoth went back to Lurgent, examining a handful of cartridges as he walked. He seemed to doubt that the cartridges were genuine. Just to make certain, he fired the revolver at the ground. He scowled in astonishment at a hole the bullet made.

"Them guys must've had a bulletproof car!" he muttered.

Lurgent cleared his throat. He wore the expression of a man in the middle of a bad dream.

"What the blazes ails *you*?" asked Behemoth.

Lurgent rubbed his forehead with palm. He didn't say anything.

"A fine brave bunch of mugs you turned out to be!" Behemoth said scathingly to Lurgent and his men.

Lurgent croaked. "Didn't you recognize those five men?"

"Huh."

"I didn't think you did!" Lurgent said grimly.

"Whatcha mean?"

"Those five—with one exception—are the five most dangerous men you could probably find."

Behemoth looked bewildered. "I don't get you."

"*They were Doc Savage's five assistants!*" Lurgent said grimly.

Chapter V

THE IDEA MAN

Lurgent lost no time in getting his men away from the vicinity of the inlet. Lurgent's first terror wore off, and was replaced with a grim seriousness. They rode in two cars, with both Behemoth and Lurgent in the lead machine. There were three others in this car, and all but Behemoth looked as if they were coming from a funeral. Behemoth showed no concern, and seemed amused by the long faces. He fell to chuckling.

"This Doc Savage seems to have an Indian sign on you fellows," he said.

Lurgent looked at Behemoth disgustedly. "It must be your ignorance! Haven't you ever heard of Doc Savage?"

"Sure. Just a guy who helps people, ain't he? Kind of a philanthropist."

"Philanthropist!" Lurgent groaned. "That's what I thought! It's not bravery! It's stupidity!"

"Whether I got brains or not is a matter of opinion," Behemoth muttered.

Approaching their tourist-camp hideout, the men became cautious and looked about for traces of ambush.

Behemoth, watching them curiously, seemed to become infected with their uneasy virus, and muttered, "You don't expect to see Doc Savage around here?"

"Oh, pipe down!" Lurgent snapped. "If you knew anything about this bronze man, you wouldn't be so cocky!"

"Bronze man?"

"That's what they call Doc Savage," Lurgent growled.

Satisfied that no menace to themselves lurked in the vicinity, the group entered the tourist cabin where the girl was being held. Behemoth threw away his chewed cigar stub and substituted a fresh weed.

Lurgent said, "Drive one of the cars up to the side door. Roll that girl in a blanket and put her in the machine. The rest of you get ready to leave here."

The men collected their belongings; in a few minutes they entered the cars, and the machines rolled away.

"Where we goin'?" Behemoth wanted to know.

Lurgent frowned at him. "There's a lot you ain't wise to yet."

Behemoth did not appear offended.

"This looks like a good job to me. That green guy Vesterate, or whatever his name is, sure puzzles me. Who is he anyway?"

"What do I look like, a mind reader?" Lurgent growled.

Behemoth flicked some ashes out a window. "Seeing you're the boss I thought you might know."

Lurgent scowled. "Sometimes you get in my hair," he admitted sourly. "Don't you ever do anything but ask questions?"

Behemoth overlooked the sarcasm in the other's voice.

"There's only one more thing I'd like to know," he said. "What did those fellows clean things back in the cabin for?"

Lurgent seemed about to explode, but managed to calm down.

"You probably wouldn't know if I told you!" he gritted. "We ain't taking chances on leaving fingerprints, that's all. Only a dumb ox like you wouldn't know that!"

"I wouldn't say I was dumb," Behemoth came back. "I'm just naturally curious, that's all."

"It's a bad disease to have," Lurgent pointed out meaningly. Something in his voice made the driver shudder. Behemoth obviously didn't catch the hidden meaning. He settled back, seeming to enjoy his cigar. He looked larger than either of the two men in the car.

The cars traveled at a moderate pace, carefully obeying traffic rules. Making a left turn, the little cavalcade proceeded along a road where there was much less traffic, and then took an even more deserted road, finally turning into a farmyard.

Their destination presented all the outward appearances of

a modest country estate of a gentleman of small means. The buildings were ancient, but had been kept up; the house was white clapboard, and the barn was of stone, with a shingled roof.

Two people appeared—perfect farmer types. The lady was elderly, wrinkled and wearing gingham. The old gentleman chewed tobacco and wore overalls.

"You stupid apes!" the nice-looking old lady yelled. "You should have better gumption than to bring such a mob here!"

She was obviously a man in masquerade.

"Shut up!" Lurgent said. "Hell has broke loose. We have to contact the Man on the Moon without fooling around."

They entered the old farmhouse. Behemoth took notice that there was an extremely modern-looking radio aerial atop the farmhouse.

A youngish-looking fellow met them inside.

"Get us through!" Lurgent said. "This is important."

The young man led them into an adjacent room. Here stood radio transmitting and receiving equipment which was obviously powerful and modern. A placard over the equipment bore a set of call letters such as are assigned to amateur radio stations.

The young man threw switches and adjusted knobs, then picked up a hand microphone.

"Calling CQ!" he said into the mike. "Station X9BJG in the hills of Virginia is calling CQ! Hello CQ!"

"Hello, X9BJG," came out of the receiver loudspeaker. "Station X21AR hooking up with X9BJG. You getting me, old man?"

Behemoth took his cigar out of his mouth. His interest was almost childish.

"Greetings and salutations, X21AR," said the young man at the farmhouse. "Boy, you're putting through a nice signal this morning. QSA five, R nine!"

This was the accepted technique by which a radio amateur operator let any other ham know that he wanted to start a conversation. But the young man here in the farmhouse did not move his receiving dial in search of a reply; instead, he set the dial at a specific point—obviously he was expecting an answer on a definite wave length.

This technical conversation continued for minutes; then the young operator in the farmhouse winked at Lurgent.

"Look, old man, my modulating circuit seems to have a bug in it," he said into his microphone. "If you hear funny noises you'll know what it is. Stand by a minute, will you, then give me a report."

He opened a large suitcase which proved to be full of apparatus, and connected this to his transmitter, then plugged his microphone into the new apparatus and began to talk.

"Lurgent is here with something important to report," he said. "I'll put him on the air."

Lurgent looked doubtful. "You sure nobody will overhear that?"

The young man pointed at the apparatus. "That's a scrambler. On the air there's just a roaring noise like a feedback in the oscillator. The other station picks it up and unscrambles it. Nobody will understand you"—he laughed—"except X21AR."

Lurgent pointed at Behemoth. "You get out!" He jerked his jaw at the others. "You too! This conversation won't suffer for privacy."

Behemoth was obviously reluctant, but he followed the others outside, and they closed the door, then stood there, the men lighting cigarettes and Behemoth puffing his inevitable cigar. They could hear no word of what was being said over the radio.

One of the men spoke idly to Behemoth. "I'd be careful about crossing Lurgent, big boy. He's not just one of the small-time straw bosses."

Behemoth grinned amiably. "Say, I'm a new man in this outfit. Fact is, I've only been in the gang since the day before yesterday. Up in New York, I heard through some connections of mine that a bird named Lurgent had some work for a few right guys. He was only hirin' birds who had hitched in the navy in Europe, and had served some time in submarines. So I come to see Lurgent, and he asks me some questions, and I show him some newspaper clips of my tough record, and he hires me."

Behemoth paused to sigh deeply and shake his head. "Lurgent brings us all south, and says we're heading for Norfolk to pull a job tomorrow. He don't say what the job is, but he acts kind of mysterious. And then, all of a sudden, as if he had got word something had gone wrong, Lurgent brings us up here and we wait near that Spanish Plantation, and we see a funny light in the sky which seems to land near that inlet. We go over there, and we run into crazy talk about a man from the moon, and such stuff."

Behemoth shrugged his huge shoulders. "You know, all this has got me plumb fizzy-giggled."

"Eh?"

"Fizzy-giggled," Behemoth explained. "Man, when I'm that way, I really don't know whether I'm goin' or comin'! Look, pal, do you know what any of this crazy business is about?"

"Just that Lurgent was tryin' to stop the green man from reachin' that girl."

"Why?"

"How should I know? I haven't been with this crew longer than you have. Lurgent hired me in New York too."

"You an ex-navy man?"

"Sure. Submarines. But I'm no more on this than you are."

Behemoth heaved in a great sigh. "Me, I'm goin' to do my best to find out what's going on here."

A few moments later Lurgent appeared, his face grim, and gave Behemoth a fierce glare.

"Orders are to kill that girl," he said.

Behemoth blinked.

"What's the idea?" he wanted to know.

"We've got to wipe out every trace of what's happened to-night," Lurgent retorted. "That's orders. Get the girl."

Behemoth looked disappointed. "Daggone it. I guess I'll have to tell the rest of the story."

"What story?"

"That girl," Behemoth muttered, "is one of Doc Savage's helpers."

"You're crazy as—" Lurgent launched forward suddenly and seized fistfuls of Behemoth's shirt. "*What*!"

"This girl talked to me," Behemoth said. "She told quite a story. Have you ever heard of Patricia Savage?"

"Patricia Savage?" Lurgent crashed a fist into his palm. "Crawling snakes! Is this girl Pat Savage?"

Behemoth took his cigar out of his mouth, looked at it and seemed very pleased with himself.

"Sure," he said. "Now we've got bait."

"What?"

"Use your head!" Behemoth said. "We let this girl over-hear enough to make her believe that our big boss will meet us at a certain spot at a certain time. Then we let her go. She takes word of the meeting to Doc Savage. He comes to grab the chief. We're ready for Doc. It's a trap, see?"

Lurgent licked his lips. "What provoked all that brainwork, Behemoth?"

Behemoth said, "I'm ambitious—maybe."

Lurgent thought that over and finally threw his hands up in defeat. "Come on into the radio room."

Wearing his proudest expression, Behemoth went in and seated himself before the radio transmitter. He seemed nervous and unaccustomed to the microphone at first and made the mistake of holding it too close to his mouth and shouting, until the operator hurriedly moved the microphone about a foot and cautioned Behemoth to use an ordinary tone. Behemoth then told the microphone about the same story he had given Lurgent.

Then the operator threw a switch and a strange, hollow voice came out of the speaker.

"You have an excellent plan, Behemoth," it said. "Examining my record here, I find that you are a new man in our organization. I like this early ingenuity that you are displaying."

Behemoth winked triumphantly at Lurgent, who glared.

Then the voice over the radio outlined a deft and brilliant plan.

"And I shall personally supervise the taking of Doc Savage," the voice finished.

"You're coming here?" Lurgent asked.

"Yes."

That ended the radio exchange.

Something like an hour later, they began the operation of setting the trap for Doc Savage. Lurgent and Behemoth, standing beside the girl, staged a conversation which they had rehearsed earlier. The exchange was rambling and natural, and the gist of it was that their leader was to arrive at this spot to consult with them a few hours hence. Proceeding with the second part of the plan, Lurgent ordered that the girl was to die immediately. Behemoth made it clear he would do the job.

"Put her in a car, and dump her over by Washington somewhere," Lurgent directed. "We don't want the body found around here."

"You bet!" agreed Behemoth.

Lifting the young woman, Behemoth carried her easily out to one of the cars and placed her in the rear seat.

Easing his huge frame behind the wheel, Behemoth drove off. He drove at a slow pace for a good reason: it enabled him to take a cellophone wrapper off one of his cigars. Then he pulled one of the buttons off his rough shirt, and used it to make marks on the cellophane—these weren't exactly marks, for the buttons left no traces visible to an unaided eye. If this note could have been read, the reader would have found:

> FAKING LETTING A GIRL ESCAPE FROM ME ON
> ROAD BACK OF FARM. GET THERE AND MARK
> SPOT. TAKE GIRL AND QUESTION HER. WHAT
> IS BEHIND THIS THING IS STILL A MYSTERY.

For several miles, Behemoth drove. Eventually he passed a farmhouse, and beside the road near this farmhouse lay two rabbits which might have been hit by cars. Behemoth tossed the note out here.

Driving on slowly, he killed some time, then took a road to the right and slowly circled back on a side road which passed to the rear of the farmhouse where he had just dropped the note. Immediately he stopped.

It was late morning now and the air was pleasant; there were feathery clouds above and enough breeze was stirring to shake the leaves of the thick brush which grew alongside the road.

Behemoth got out, opened the rear door, seized the girl's feet and yanked. One of her slippers came off, apparently by accident, and he stumbled back with it in his hand.

The ropes on the girl's ankles seemed loose, and came free with her slipper. Instantly she leaped from the other side of the car.

Behemoth went "*Whoosh!*"—the nearest he could come to a shout. He stumbled around the car. The girl was scrambling across the roadside into the brush. Behemoth rushed after her, stubbed his toe, turned a somersault and crashed flat on his back in the ditch.

He lay there for a few moments, as if stunned. Then he got up and began searching for the girl, shoving through brush noisily. However, he deliberately passed up the young woman's trail when he located it. Finally he ran back to the car, got in and drove away.

Returning to the isolated farmhouse radio station, he told Lurgent, "Figure I should've been an actor."

"It went off all right?" Lurgent asked.

"Sure!"

"I'll see about that." Lurgent went over and kicked the trunk at the rear of the car. The trunk lid opened and one of Lurgent's men, who had been concealed within, got out.

"He went through with it exactly like he was told to do it," the stowaway said.

Behemoth seemed about to explode with anger, but eventually he cooled off and shrugged. "Well, the girl will go straight to Doc Savage," he said. "And when she tells Savage her story, he'll come here, and we'll fix things up nicely."

Chapter VI

THE FOX

Lin Pretti had not gone far. In fact, seeking to escape Behemoth, she had climbed a huge tree which had small branches growing almost the whole length of its trunk, which made it easy to mount. High up in the tree was a cavity, entirely invisible from the ground, into which she was able to insert her slender form. Such an excellent hiding place, she was reluctant to desert, at least until Behemoth stopped searching.

After almost an hour, she concluded her pursuer had departed. Seeing nothing to worry her, she descended. Once on the ground, she rearranged her clothing.

"I've been lucky!" she exclaimed softly.

"Probably luckier than you deserve!" said a small childlike voice.

Lin Pretti jumped and spun. Out from behind the tree she had just descended—he must have crept up silently on the other side of the tree—appeared a remarkable-looking fellow.

The resemblance this newcomer bore to an amiable ape was striking. He was nearly as broad as tall, had an enormous mouth, small deep-set eyes and almost no forehead. He was so incredibly homely in such a pleasant fashion that Lin Pretti's first impulse was to smile.

"I've been waiting for you," the homely apparition explained.

"Oh!" ejaculated Lin Pretti.

Then her eyes rested on a strange animal which had followed the homely man. This was a pig. The shote had long thin legs, a pair of tremendously long ears, and a snout built for inquisitiveness.

A second man appeared from the brush. This stranger was slender, especially at the waist, and his clothing was almost foppishly immaculate, and of a pattern distinctly unusual, consisting of spats, striped trousers, gray lap-over vest, cutaway coat, wing collar, and Ascot tie. He carried a black sword cane.

"I don't blame you for being scared," he told Lin Pretti pleasantly, with a meaning glance at the homely man. "A number of people have had to go to bed after their first look at Monk, here."

"Ham, you overdressed shyster!" the apish Monk growled.

"You mistake-that-nature-made!" the too well-dressed man retorted.

Then the two stuck out their jaws and glared at each other.

Lin Pretti gasped, "Who are you?"

"I am Brigadier General Theodore Marley Brooks," said the perfectly clad man.

"Call him Ham!" snorted the homely Monk. "Everybody else does."

The violence of Brigadier General Theodore Marley Brooks' grimace indicated he did not care for the nickname.

"What do you want with me?" the girl asked.

"Information," Monk said. "Come on."

Shortly afterward, Lin Pretti found herself approaching a farmhouse—the one in front of which Behemoth had dropped his note but she did not know that. It was painted brown, with rose bushes in the yard and an automobile standing under a tree. There was a barn in the back, and behind the barn—where its presence became known only after one entered the yard—stood two airplanes; two small, fast amphibians.

The weeds in the yard stirred, drawing Lin Pretti's attention. At first she thought she was seeing some kind of grotesque dwarf. An animal, though, when she corrected her first impression—some type of chimpanzee, or small baboon. The chimpanzee was striking because of the resemblance in miniature which it bore to the homely Monk.

"Chemistry!" called the well-dressed Ham. The animal came swinging happily toward him. "My pet," he told Lin Pretti.

Monk, not to be outdone, indicated the pig with the big ears and long legs. "That's *my* pet, named Habeas Corpus," he said proudly.

Chemistry and Habeas began showing their teeth in a manner which indicated they got along about as truculently as did their respective owners.

A young woman, a particularly striking young woman, greeted them when they entered the house. She was tall and exquisitely molded; her hair was of an unusual bronze hue, and her eyes were amazingly like pools of flake gold.

Lin Pretti looked at this second young woman. Something seemed to strike her.

"Oh!" she gasped. "I've seen—your picture in the newspapers!"

"I'm Patricia Savage," said the young woman.

Lin Pretti gasped. "Doc Savage . . ."

"Is my cousin," Patricia Savage finished. "Sit down. We want to talk to you."

Lin Pretti said defiantly, "Let me go!"

Pat Savage stepped to her, shoved, and Lin Pretti sat down ignominiously.

"No, Pat!" Monk said. "You're too enthusiastic."

"You bet," Pat said. "I've been so long without excitement that I can't restrain myself. I'll probably box this hussy's ears. Hold her, Monk."

Both Monk and Ham showed eagerness to hold Lin Pretti. They each got one of the pretty prisoner's arms and glared at each other.

Pat told Lin Pretti, "You had better start talking."

Lin Pretti shook her head. "I've nothing to say."

"Just on the chance that it might loosen your tongue," Pat stated, "I'm going to explain our position in this."

Monk blurted, "Pat . . ."

"Let me do this," Pat directed him. Then to Lin Pretti, "You know something about Doc Savage, don't you?"

"No."

"I wish you wouldn't start lying to me," Pat complained. "You had a young man by the name of Bob Thomas make some inquiries about Doc."

Lin Pretti looked startled.

"You see," Pat elaborated, "when your Bob Thomas started making inquiries, it came to our notice. We learned that Bob Thomas was being very attentive to you, and it occurred to us that he might be getting the information for you."

Lin Pretti shuddered. "What brought Doc Savage into this?"

Pat glanced at Monk. "Show her that clipping, Monk."

The homely Monk hesitated. "Now, I don't know if we ought."

"It's no secret," Pat reminded him. "The newspapers published it, didn't they?"

The clipping was in French. Translated, it read:

DOC SAVAGE DIRIGIBLE
CRUISES FRANCE

A private dirigible, owned by Doc Savage, has been cruising over French territory, it became known today after French military planes had forced the craft to land for examination.

As soon as it was ascertained that the dirigible belonged to Doc Savage, it was allowed to proceed. It had been halted because it was over territory prohibited to foreign fliers.

French officials have apologized for the incident.

Doc Savage, because of services rendered in the past to the French government, is accorded special exemption from all ordinary regulations.

It was evident Lin Pretti could read French fluently; she looked up from the item, plainly puzzled. "Well, what of it?"

"That wasn't Doc's dirigible," Pat Savage explained. "When Doc heard about it, he sent Colonel John Renwick to France to investigate. Renny is one of Doc's five assistants. Renwick got on the trail of one of the fellows who had been on that dirigible. Renny's quarry was a man named Donald Lurgent. Renny trailed Donald Lurgent to the United States."

Lin Pretti was staring, her eyes very wide.

Pat continued, "When Lurgent got to New York, he immediately hired a gang of crooks. He seemed to need a particular kind of crook—men who had served in the navy of some country, always in the submarine service. What do you know about that, young lady?"

Lin Pretti shook her head mutely.

Pat said, "Lurgent brought his men down here. They were going to Norfolk to pull some kind of job tomorrow. We haven't been able to learn what the job tomorrow may be. But tonight Lurgent got a hurry call and brought his men to a spot near the Spanish Plantation, where they watched the sky. What do you know about that?"

"Nothing," Lin Pretti said defiantly.

The dapper Ham said, "Then we're all even. Nobody knows anything."

"Yeah," grunted homely Monk. "And let me show you what mystifies us most."

The homely fellow took Lin Pretti's elbow and guided her into an adjacent room. On the threshold the girl started and gave a gasp of surprise. This outburst was caused by a figure which lay on a bed in the room.

It was the green man. His wounds had been bandaged.

"Who is this freak?" Ham asked Lin Pretti.

The girl grabbed her lower lip with her teeth. She did not speak.

"The fellow muttered some stuff about having been to the moon," Ham said. "And he muttered some more junk about a little blue capsule. What did he mean?"

Emotion—it certainly looked like terror—seemed to weaken Lin Pretti, and Monk quickly supported her with an arm.

Pat snapped at the girl, "Talk up! What is this all about?"

Lin Pretti mumbled. "I can't—won't—" She said no more.

Pat said, "Come on! Was that man really on the moon?"

Lin Pretti sighed, and her head sagged forward.

"She's fainted!" Monk yelled.

"Darn!" Ham complained. "She would faint on us!" He indicated the green man. "He's unconscious; the girl won't talk; how are we going to get information?"

Monk said, "I guess we'll have to rely on Lurgent's moves to clear this up."

Chapter VII

THE UNDECEIVED

Donald Lurgent had misplaced his hat somewhere, and was hunting it, swearing profusely. His humor was vicious.

Behemoth, the giant who admitted he was ambitious, was wetting one of his cigars with his tongue, preparatory to lighting it. He seemed quite pleased with himself and, as usual, was asking questions with childlike curiosity.

The trap for Doc Savage was being set. Lurgent made a little speech to make sure that everyone understood the plan.

To this lecture the huge, cigar-smoking Behemoth listened intently. Then he asked in his strange whisper, "If this Doc Savage is such a holy terror, why don't this Man on the Moon have us just clear out and leave Savage alone?"

"You're getting my goat!" Lurgent came over and poked a stiff forefinger against Behemoth's chest. "Now get this, and get it straight! I'm a small cog in this thing, and you're a damn sight smaller! I've told you that the Man on the Moon has something big to pull tomorrow morning. Savage is monkeying around. We can't take any chances with that bronze fellow."

"Sure, but what is this thing tomorrow . . ."

"I don't ask questions, and I don't try to push my ideas where they're not wanted. My advice to you, ugly and troublesome, is to follow the same system."

"I got more ambition than some guys," Behemoth explained.

"Some sense would get you farther."

Behemoth scratched his head. "The things that feller in the queer green suit, Tony Vesterate or whatever his name is, said about being to the moon sure interests me."

Lurgent scowled. "Forget that! Don't let me hear you mention it again!"

"But everybody thinks the moon ain't inhabited . . ."

"Shut up! No more about that—you hear?"

"Aw, have a heart. On account of this mysterious business tomorrow, you've taken on new men, of which I'm one. And it ain't no more than fair to tell me what we're doing tomorrow so . . ."

"Except for one thing, I'd kick you out of this thing!" Lurgent snarled.

"Brother, if you feel that way, go ahead," Behemoth shrugged. "I'm not a boy who has trouble getting jobs. Anyway, I think I've got brains. The Man on the Moon seems to think so too."

Lurgent rubbed his jaw and looked dark. "Maybe we can tell the Man on the Moon to just leave the skull work to you, big-simple!"

Behemoth grinned. "Jealous? Or do you just like to razz guys?"

"You know too much."

"Eh?"

"There's only one way of canning you now!" Lurgent drew a pistol from one pocket, fingered it meaningly, and put it back.

"Think it over," he said.

Behemoth then started mumbling about being an honest, ambitious fellow just trying to get ahead in the world without stepping on any toes, and could he help it if he had a well-developed bump of curiosity, and wasn't it a fine business to be threatened just because he was curious about tomorrow . . .

"You'll get that curiosity bump knocked off if you don't pipe down!" Lurgent snarled.

"Am I gonna see the boss—this Man on the Moon?" Behemoth whispered with sudden violence.

"You'll see him," Lurgent said queerly.

A truck arrived at that point. It was an ordinary-looking vehicle with a common variety of trunk in the rear, covered with a canvas. The two drivers of the vehicle began unloading the trunk, but worked very slowly, and with what seemed to be reluctance. Their lack of enthusiasm immediately aggravated Behemoth.

He strode over and seized the trunk. "Lemme show you guys how a *man* does things!"

The two truckmen gasped, fright washed color off their faces, and they whirled as if to run. Donald Lurgent sprang forward wildly to shove Behemoth back from the trunk.

"You idiot!" he screeched. "That thing is full of TNT!"

"Uh—whooey!" Behemoth jumped away from the trunk, ran to a nearby ditch and dived into its shelter. There was a great deal of laughter at the big fellow's expense.

The trunk of violent explosive was carried into the farmhouse.

From conversation, Behemoth now learned that the trunk also held a radio-electrical device—an ingenious contraption by which a radio signal could be transmitted from a distant point to a receiving set in the trunk, which would cause a relay to close, completing a circuit that set off a detonator and would explode the trunk's contents.

Behemoth fearfully inquired about the probable violence of the blast. He was told that the entire top of the hill would be demolished.

It was also explained to Behemoth that Lurgent and the Man on the Moon would watch this farmhouse from the peak of a small nearby mountain, observe Doc Savage enter the farmhouse, then explode the TNT.

"From what mountain will we watch?" Behemoth inquired.

Lurgent pointed. "There, stupid!"

It was a tall, rocky and thickly wooded hill about three miles distant. It was also the highest hill in the vicinity, and a highway, or parts of it, could be distinguished winding up to the top of the eminence.

"Nice lookout place," Behemoth agreed.

A few moments later, Behemoth got into one of the empty cars, ostensibly to await the departure. He drew out a fresh cigar, stripped off the cellophane, and pulled another of the buttons off his own coat. He was very careful that no one saw him.

Spreading the cellophane out, he proceeded to make letters on the cellophane. The letters were, of course, invisible to the unaided eye. Behemoth was careful to keep the lines straight and form each letter carefully, making the communication read:

> TRAP IS EXPLOSIVE IN FARMHOUSE. WILL BE
> SET OFF BY RADIO FROM TOP OF MOST PROM-
> INENT MOUNTAIN. MOUNTAIN IS FOUR MILES
> WEST. MAN ON MOON WILL BE THERE. TAKE
> THEM. BE CAREFUL. THEY ARE DANGEROUS.

Behemoth folded this missive into a tiny pellet, then inserted it in the end of the cigar he had been smoking—the chewed end. The cigar had gone out. He was careful not to relight it.

In a short time, Donald Lurgent and the others completed the planting of the explosive and got into the automobiles. The machines drove down the road.

Less than a mile from the farmhouse trap, the machines passed two rabbits which lay in the road, where they might have been run over by cars.

Behemoth calmly threw his chewed cigar stub away at that point.

The fragment of cigar bounced into the grader ditch, where it lay in plain sight on some sand.

A man detached himself from the concealment of a nearby tree, approached the road, picked up the two rabbits and dropped them in a large inside pocket with which his brown hunting coat was equipped.

This man was at least a foot taller than an average man, and he looked as if he were fully a hundred pounds underweight. He was, in fact, thinner than it seemed any man could be and still remain healthy. His shoulders, under his coat, resembled a wooden coat hanger. A monocle was attached by a cord to his coat lapel.

He dug the bit of cellophane out of the cigar stub. From his pocket he took one of the small devices which resembled a diminutive box camera, except that it had a dark glass lens. Smoothing the cellophane out, he made an impromptu darkroom inside his coat, turned the device on, and the message sprang out in its eerie phosphorescence.

"I'll be superamalgamated!" said the thin man, having read.

He stowed the note and the device in his coat, strode out through the woods, taking long steps, his head back. A low-hanging branch snagged his monocle cord, and he carefully tucked the monocle into his breast pocket.

When he looked up from replacing the monocle, it was to see a man standing in an open glade in front of him with a rifle. It was one of Lurgent's men.

"Well, well," this fellow said bitterly.

The thin man with the monocle crouched, obviously about to chance a dive for concealment. But two other men came out on either side, also with rifles. Like the first, they were Lurgent's men.

"I'll be superamalgamated!" gasped the tall man.

One of Lurgent's fellows nodded. "Yep, that long word proves who he is. He's William Harper Littlejohn, sometimes known as Johnny. He's one of Doc Savage's five assistants."

"*What?*"

"Whew!" the third man said soberly. "We may not have much time to lose!"

They hurried William Harper Littlejohn—Johnny—through the woods, saying very little after they had searched him. Johnny said little, for there obviously wasn't any use. They were Lurgent's men, but how had they gotten on his trail? Surely it wasn't an accident.

A casual remark answered that question. The men, it seemed, had been put out to carefully comb the surrounding woodland just as a general precautionary measure. Lurgent's suspicions of Behemoth had continued, hence the search. And, too, the hunt had been motivated by the remarkable amount of apprehension created by discovery of the fact that Doc Savage was investigating the Man on the Moon and the rest of the strange mystery.

Johnny's captors reached a side road, where the prisoner was placed on his back, and his wrists and ankles were securely lashed with a stout cord. One of the men produced a roll of friction tape, and pieces of this were crisscrossed over Johnny's eyes until there was no possibility of him seeing anything.

One of the men departed. He must have gone to summon individuals in an automobile, because the machine arrived shortly.

"It's the Man on the Moon!" gasped one of Johnny's captors in a startled whisper.

Johnny's bony length stiffened. The mastermind here? He was supposed to join Lurgent on the mountaintop! What had gone wrong? But how could they suspect when they hadn't read the message on that bit of cellophane?

"The box is a tiny projector of ultraviolet light," said the Man on the Moon. "Certain substances glow, or phosphoresce, when exposed to ultraviolet light. Common aspirin is an example. But there are others. Look for secret writing."

They found it on the cellophane, and read it aloud.

"It's the damned Behemoth who's double-crossing us!" a man barked.

"We'll take care of Behemoth," said the Man on the Moon. "We were very fortunate to discover this."

Johnny, straining to recognize the speaker's voice, was defeated. Likewise he could identify no peculiarities by which he could identify the speaker later. But the fellow was evidently no supernatural being, except for being far more clever than Johnny had hoped.

The Man on the Moon's voice was unnatural, many of the words imperfectly formed, and Johnny, who was an expert at disguising his own voice, decided the man was holding a silver dollar on edge between his teeth—or some similar object. That, with a little change in tone, would disguise any voice.

"An ultra-acrimonious consequentiality," Johnny said disgustedly.

"Whoo!" a man said. "Such words!"

"Contumacious obstinacy permeates me," Johnny mumbled.

A man said, "Make him talk English."

"Let him talk anything as long as he talks," said the hollow voice.

Johnny was kicked again, was directed, "Spill!"

Shock seemed to explode inside Johnny's head, hurl his consciousness high up in vagueness. Painfully his mind cleared, and he realized he had been kicked on the temple.

"Talk!" directed the Man on the Moon. "Where is Doc Savage?"

"Hell with you!" Johnny gasped.

He was kicked again, but more as a gesture, then there were low orders, and a man growled, "Too bad if you've got adenoids," and began sticking strips of adhesive tape over Johnny's mouth.

"He'll probably wish he could smother himself," said the unnatural voice of the leader, "before we're done with him."

Johnny was heaved into a smooth-sounding car.

"Go tell Lurgent to take Behemoth," one of the men was ordered.

Chapter VIII

FANTASTIC IS TOMORROW

The courier bearing orders to Donald Lurgent raced through the wooded hills until he reached a spot where he had a small car concealed. He drove this machine rapidly to the mountaintop.

Once he almost ran off the road, for he was devoting much time to staring about anxiously in search of some trace of Doc Savage. He was nervous, and at times it seemed he was going to eat his own lips, so fearfully did he bite them. He had plainly heard of Doc Savage, and considered the man of bronze a grim menace to himself. He even muttered profanely, demanding to know why in hades any man should make a career of "monkeying with things that ain't any of his business!"

The courier scowled. He was remembering how Behemoth had pried into everything with childlike curiosity. They had just thought the big fellow was a little stupid and nosy. They hadn't dreamed that a spy would be so openly nosy. This Behemoth was really a clever devil.

The tip of the mountain was wooded, except for one bald spot. Donald Lurgent and his men had parked their cars near this, behind some small trees. They had spread a few blankets out on the ground and placed a basket of food in a prominent spot to give the resemblance of a picnic to anyone who passed.

The messenger stopped his machine. Almost the first person he saw was huge cigar-smoking Behemoth.

"Anything new on what we're to do tomorrow?" Behemoth whispered hopefully.

Pretending to glower angrily at the big fellow, the messenger compared Behemoth with what he had heard of Doc Savage's five assistants. All five were distinctive in appearance. Behemoth was certainly not one of them.

"You've been told not to ask so damn many questions!" the man grated.

He strode on, hunting Lurgent. He heard Behemoth ambling after him, and the flesh on his back seemed to crawl.

The gang would kill Behemoth, of course. He had come to tell Lurgent to do that. Suddenly he decided that, if Behemoth stopped and turned his back, he himself would put a bullet into the big fellow.

Behemoth stopped. The messenger put a hand in a pocket which held a gun and wheeled. But Behemoth was facing him, and he didn't quite dare.

"Where's Lurgent?" he snarled.

"Over there." Behemoth indicated a bush.

The courier found Lurgent. He glanced back, and perceived the huge Behemoth had a pair of binoculars to his eyes and was staring toward the distant mined farmhouse. The messenger jerked in a sigh of relief.

"Don't show any surprise," he growled at Lurgent. "I've got some damn bad news."

Lurgent glowered down his beak of a nose. The strain of waiting had him in a bad temper.

"Shoot!" he snapped.

The courier shot his news, explaining exactly how it had become known that Behemoth was passing information to Doc Savage's aides.

"What he's trying to do is find out about this business tomorrow," the man finished.

Lurgent glanced covertly at Behemoth, saw the big man with the binoculars still to his eyes.

"Damn him!" Lurgent almost strangled. "The ugly skunk slicked us properly! Asked questions and pried and cut up until I just thought he was nutty."

Lurgent pinched his eyes shut, made a fierce face and went on, "Now I know why we had so much bad luck!" His face turned purple and he made choking noises. "I wonder—oh, hell! *Was that girl really Pat Savage?*"

"*Sh-h-h!*" warned the courier. "He may wonder what's giving you spasms."

Lurgent gurgled, he was so angry. "If he's found out what our real business is—about the men on the moon—about—but he couldn't have! He couldn't! I've kept my mouth shut! But—well, damn him! We'll soon fix his pie!"

They glanced toward Behemoth again. But he was lowering his binoculars and turning away. He disappeared, leisurely, in the brush.

Behemoth's appearance of lazy unconcern vanished the instant he was concealed in the bushes. He tossed the binoculars aside; they had served his purpose.

Behemoth happened to be a skilled lip reader. And he had not been watching the distant farmhouse; that was only pretense. He had employed the glasses on Lurgent and the courier, and learned almost all that they said.

Whipping to the left, he used all his strange ability to move with ghostly silence. His objective—the point where Lurgent and the messenger stood—he reached quickly. But Lurgent had moved.

The courier still stood there, however. He held his revolver in his hand, was plainly nervous.

Behemoth remained hidden, silent, watchful. He saw Lurgent. The man was plainly making the rounds of his followers, warning them.

From inside his garments Behemoth drew a small case. Out of this came small objects which resembled glass marbles at first glance. Actually these things were glass spheroids containing an uncolored liquid. He threw one.

The thin glass struck beside the messenger, broke, and he looked down. He blinked his eyes, looked suddenly utterly sleepy, peered at the ground as if hunting a place to sleep, and lay down heavily without finding it.

Behemoth had held his breath since he threw the ball. He now hurled others—far, high. They shattered near Lurgent's men. Lurgent whirled. He must have seen one of them break. He certainly knew what it was—a colorless, odorless anesthetic gas producing instant harmless unconsciousness, perfected by Doc Savage and long used by those associated with the man of bronze.

Lurgent knew its nature, for he did the one thing that saved him. He held his breath. The vapor, mixing with the air, became ineffective in a few moments.

Lurgent ran. The cars were not far from him; he made for them.

Behemoth suddenly raced to head him off. His speed, for a human, was almost incredible. But Lurgent was far nearer the cars, and not slow either. Lurgent also had a gun. He whipped it out, began firing. Menace of the bullets drove Behemoth behind trees.

Lurgent piled into a car, started the motor. Then he drove wildly down the mountainside.

Behemoth, left behind, was in control of the situation. Lurgent had fled.

There were, however, some survivors; three men in all who had been acting as lookouts on the other side of the mountain. They came sidling out of the brush, alarmed by the shots, guns ready.

Behemoth strolled boldly toward them, wearing a big grin.

"It's all over," he said amiably.

"What—what—who . . ."

"Lurgent," Behemoth said, "got all finished here and left."

"You mean he got Doc Savage?" one of the trio yelled. He popped his eyes at the motionless gas victims. "What—why —it must've happened like lightning!"

"It sure did. Lurgent was right excited when he left."

"He took Doc Savage away?"

Behemoth didn't exactly affirm this. But he grinned.

"Lurgent left me in charge," he said.

Which was the literal truth.

The three men, not particularly brilliant, were deceived, and accepted the fact that Behemoth was now to be their chief. They nodded, wide-eyed.

"The car tires got punctured," Behemoth explained. "You'd better change them."

Firing at Behemoth, Lurgent had deliberately punctured the tires of the remaining cars.

The three dupes set about this task. Behemoth stood nearby, wearing his big amiable grin, the perfect picture of a pleasant dunce who had just been promoted to a better job.

The tire changers excitedly wanted to know what Doc Savage had looked like. Behemoth glibly described a man with skin of remarkable bronze hue and strange flake-gold eyes. He ended this recital by voicing a personal opinion that Doc Savage was overrated and some day bound to bite off more than he could chew.

"I'm a new member of Lurgent's gang," Behemoth remarked finally. "I don't know much about what we're doing."

"Lurgent ain't the main man," one of the trio reminded.

"Sure he isn't. I know that, boys. What you're to tell me is who we're really working for."

"The Man on the Moon."

"Sure. But who is it calls himself by that goofy name?"

They said they didn't know.

Behemoth shrugged. "Where is he from?"

They said they had the impression he was pretty much from everywhere, but they didn't know exactly where.

"He's got quite an organization," Behemoth suggested.

"He must have."

"What's he doing with it?"

They didn't know for sure, they said, but Lurgent had told them it was something big, something that had never been worked before, and something profitable.

Behemoth patiently angled for more information. "What is this thing we're going to pull tomorrow?"

They didn't know.

Behemoth studied them intently.

"How come you don't know anything?" he demanded.

"Why—we're new men. We joined up just a few hours before you did."

"Oh-ho!" Behemoth waved at the men who were unconscious. "How about those birds? Don't they know anything either?"

"They're new men too."

Behemoth remained expressionless. But there came upon the surrounding air, so small as to be almost unnoticeable, a trilling sound. A weird, ethereal note—musical, yet not having any tune—this rose and fell and it was particularly remarkable because there was no definite source from which it seemed to be coming, although Behemoth's lips were slightly parted.

"What's that?" a man grunted.

"Must be the voice of disappointment," Behemoth said amiably. "Look, what do you birds know about that business last night—the man who said he had been to the moon?"

"Just what Lurgent said. The man was named Tony Vesterate. And he had been on the moon and had escaped back to earth."

"Been on the moon, eh? That's nutty talk."

"That's what we thought." The man shrugged. "There isn't nothing nutty about the money we get paid, though. With what we get paid, we can do ourselves a lot of good."

"Probably more good than you think," said Behemoth.

He calmly added, "Look," broke glass balls of anesthetic under their noses, held his breath, and the men sagged over unconscious. After which Behemoth loaded them in the larger of the cars and drove away.

When Behemoth drove with his prisoners into the yard of the small farm where Patricia Savage, the homely Monk, and neatly dressed Ham were holding stubbornly silent Lin Pretti and unconscious Tony Vesterate, the man from the moon, something that he plainly didn't like caught his eye. Two rabbits lay on the road, where they might have been run over by a car.

Behemoth looked back at the rabbits. Then he stopped the car in the yard, leaped out and ran for the farmhouse door.

"Monk! Ham!" he called. "Didn't you get Johnny's note? He was to relay it—orders to go to that mountaintop!"

The door opened and Pat Savage came out. Behemoth halted precipitously.

Pat, looking especially exquisite, looked at Behemoth.

"Well, who on earth are you?" she demanded.

"Pat, you are not supposed to be here!" Behemoth said. But now Behemoth's strange whisper was gone, and he spoke in a deep, trained and unusual voice.

Pat suddenly broke into a peal of laughter. She doubled over with her mirth, slapping her knees.

"Doc!" she gasped. "Ha, ha—Doc! What kind of masquerade party have you been attending?"

The big man did not respond to her mirth. He repeated, "Did orders come here through Johnny?"

Monk ambled out on the porch, and the manner of his

walk furthered the impression of an amiable ape. Ham also appeared, neat sword cane tucked under his arm.

"Greetings, Doc," Monk said. "We didn't hear anything from Johnny."

Abruptly a tiny, trilling sound was audible. Eerie, plaintive, it seemed to have a startled quality.

"What's wrong?" Monk exploded.

"Something must have happened to Johnny!" the big man said.

They hurriedly hauled the prisoners out of the car, took them inside and bound them. Stimulants from a small case were used to revive them. As each opened his eyes, he was informed that he was in Doc Savage's hands.

The way the captives reacted to this was a tribute to the bronze man's reputation among evildoers. Their faces changed color, registering complete horror. They strained at the ropes which held them, or lay trembling.

Each of the prisoners was then taken alone into another room and given truth serum by hypodermic, after which they became stupefied and, theoretically, incapable of mumbling anything but the truth.

A number of facts were extricated.

First, these men were all American crooks hired for service in the United States.

Next, every one of them had served in a navy somewhere. Either in England, France, Russia or Italy.

While in the navy, every one of the men had put in time on submarines. It had been essential for them to be submarine men before Lurgent had enrolled them.

None of them knew much about what they were expected to do. The Man on the Moon was some kind of sinister power in the field of international affairs, some of them understood. What kind of power and what particular patch in the field of international affairs, they did not know.

Tony Vesterate, the man in green, was an earth dweller who had been taken to the moon by force, then escaped.

As for the job tomorrow, none of them had been told what it was, exactly. But it was to entail violence, include something fantastically big; each man had been warned not to be surprised at anything that might happen.

They were to assemble for the job at the Caribenna Steamship Co. pier, in Norfolk, early tomorrow morning.

William Harper Littlejohn—Johnny—had been captured by the Man on the Moon's men, and would be questioned thoroughly, then killed.

Behemoth now proceeded to cease to be Behemoth. With a chemical, he removed the rather unwholesome dye on his skin. His skin, fine-textured, became a striking bronze hue. From his lips and nostrils he took pads of flexible, adhesive composition so naturally colored that one might have looked into the mouth without recognizing them for what they were. A number of other details made up the disguise, including tinted glass caps fitting onto the eyeballs—as do the modern "invisible" eyeglasses—which changed the eye color.

Behemoth became Doc Savage, the bronze man, being of mystery, scientific genius and mental marvel, who had been trained by scientists from the cradle for the one thing he was doing now: punishing evildoers and righting wrongs.

His manner, too, changed with the assuming of Doc Savage's personality. Behemoth had been oafish, slangy, careless of his speech, slouchy of manner, free and easy and just a little of a loon.

Doc Savage had a trained, reserved, but extremely powerful personality. His eyes in particular were compelling, almost hypnotic. His carriage was erect, and also compelling. And his voice was powerful, and gave always the feeling of reserved might.

The man, Doc Savage, was striking. Even Monk and Ham —Monk, the homely fellow who was really one of the greatest living chemists, and Ham, the dapper dandy who was a great lawyer—looked at him with something of awe. And they had been with Doc Savage a long time.

Doc Savage was a physical giant—when one stood close to him. At a distance, the very symmetrical mold of his physique made it seem less gigantic. He discarded the cigars; ordinarily he did not smoke.

Doc Savage came into the room, having changed into plain dark clothing and a white shirt, but no necktie. His strange flake-gold eyes rested briefly on his cousin, Pat.

"You will be returning to New York," he said quietly.

"You can take these prisoners along, and send them on to our college."

The "college" referred to was an institution which Doc Savage maintained, unknown to the world, in upstate New York. He sent criminals here, where they underwent brain operations which deprived them of all memory of their past. Then they were trained in useful ways of making a living and released.

"I'm not going back," Pat said flatly. "I'm here, eating this up, and I'm staying!"

The bronze man's face did not change expression; he had the remarkable facility of showing emotion only when he so desired. But Monk and Ham, looking on, felt like grinning. Doc, in an amazing number of ways, was a superman. But on one point he fell somewhat short and was just like the next fellow: he couldn't outtalk a woman. Pat was buffaloing him. She had done it before.

Sure enough, Doc Savage shrugged, wheeled and walked away. He went into the next room and examined the man in the queer green suit, Tony Vesterate. The unusual garment had been removed from the victim.

"It may be two or three days before he can possibly talk," Doc Savage said. "He will be fortunate to live at all."

The bronze man worked on Vesterate's injuries for a while. Each move of the bronze man's fingers indicated some of the intensive training he had undergone in surgery. For it was in that, more than anything else, that he excelled, although he had mastered many professions to the point where he might be called an expert.

Doc Savage picked up the green suit. It had been cut partially in removing it from the wearer, and the bronze man scrutinized the cut edges with a magnifying glass.

Two new arrivals reached the farmhouse. One of these was greeted as "Renny." He was Colonel John Renwick, renowned as an engineer, and also renowned for his fists; each of his incredible hands would block out into at least a quart of knuckles. He was a big, somewhat gaunt man with a long, puritanical face which always looked as if he were taking it to someone's funeral.

The second newcomer was called "Long Tom." He was the electrical wizard of Doc's aides, full name Major Thomas J. Roberts. He was not long; that nickname had clung to him since a certain fiasco when he had tried to fire a cannon of the type known as a "Long Tom." He was a small, scrawny fellow who looked as if he had inhabited a mushroom cellar most of his life. As a matter of fact, he was perfectly healthy.

Doc Savage handed the green suit to Renny, the engineer.

Renny studied the garment. "Layers of silk, layers of composition between, probably rubber. And one layer of a fine metal mesh, possibly for strength." He fingered the metal collar of a device which encircled the shoulders, and noted the metal locknut attachments on this. "Looks as if a helmet of some kind fitted on here."

"Looks like some fantastic movie director's idea of a stratosphere suit," Long Tom offered.

"Holy cow!" Renny agreed. "It sure does." He had a great, rumbling voice.

"Did you search the inlet near which Vesterate was found, and near which that flaming meteor apparently struck?" Doc Savage inquired.

This, it developed, was what Renny and Long Tom had been doing. They mentioned that they had found the top of a tall tree scorched, as if something had passed, going toward the inlet.

The water of the inlet, they explained, became very deep a short distance offshore. There was also a rushing tide. Their efforts to search had netted nothing.

"That thing out of the sky, whatever it was, might have gone out to sea for miles—or out in Chesapeake Bay for miles, rather—before it struck," Renny rumbled.

"We searched the shoreline," Long Tom added. "I'll show you what we found."

He went out to the car in which they had arrived, came back bearing a sodden mass of very stout silk and webbing straps.

"Parachute."

Doc Savage scrutinized the straps. He found, where some of the straps had yanked hard against the form they supported as the 'chute opened, greenish stains. The parachute was also badly scorched, burned completely through at one point.

"Looks like this Vesterate bailed out of a burning thing, landed, hurt himself because the burned parachute let him down hard, then took the 'chute off and threw it in the bay."

Renny stopped his rumbling to nod soberly. "Then the parachute drifted down to where we found it."

Doc Savage agreed, "That seems logical."

"Now," Renny thumped, "this bird Lurgent expected Vesterate to arrive. Isn't that right?"

"Lurgent brought us all down from New York, where he recruited his gang, yesterday," Doc Savage admitted. "We went to Norfolk, Virginia, but got a hurry call and rushed to the neighborhood of the Spanish Plantation roadhouse, and there we all got orders to watch the sky."

Renny studied the bronze man. "What do you make of that?"

"Lurgent expected that thing to fall out of the sky at that spot. He expected Vesterate to be killed. We were there to slay Vesterate, in case he survived."

"I'm going to make a guess, Doc."

"Yes?"

"Vesterate had been a prisoner of the Man on the Moon and escaped, and they were after him."

"That is the way it appears now."

"Holy cow! This Vesterate said he had come from the moon. That's the nutty part. It's impossible!"

Long Tom, the electrical wizard, put in, "I wouldn't say it was so darned impossible. Scientists have been working hot at it for years."

"I still say it's queer," Renny rumbled.

"Here is another queer angle," Doc Savage offered. "Lurgent knew this girl, Lin Pretti, was staying near the Spanish Plantation. He knew that this man Vesterate, who came out of the sky, would try to meet her there. In other words, Vesterate had escaped from the Man on the Moon and was trying to reach Lin Pretti."

"I'm still puzzled," offered the homely Monk.

"You were born that way," the dapper Ham assured him.

Probably none of the group realized that Doc Savage had maneuvered the recent rather lengthy summary of the situation for the sole purpose of putting salient facts before them, that they might not become confused by the meaninglessness of some of the things that had happened.

It was obviously for the same purpose that Doc now reminded them they were making progress. A few weeks ago they had only known that someone was masquerading as themselves to fly freely over France and other European nations. Renny had gone to Europe, found Lurgent to be one of the masqueraders, and had followed Lurgent to New York.

True, Renny hadn't learned what mission had brought Lurgent to America, but he had learned Lurgent was recruiting a gang of aides—all with naval training—and this had given Doc Savage his opportunity to enlist in the gang. Then the trip down here, to take part in something mysterious to happen tomorrow. And the interruption of Vesterate's arrival, and what had ensued. Yes, it was progress.

But Johnny was a prisoner, and maybe dead.

A grimly silent group went in to talk to Lin Pretti.

"Remember the remarkable story you told me?" Doc asked.

The girl stared. "I've never seen you before!"

"I was Behemoth," Doc explained quietly.

Lin Pretti swallowed. Her eyes widened incredulously; she sat for some moments entirely stunned. With an effort she aroused herself and stared at the bronze man with mingled astonishment and awe. Evidently a struggle of some kind was going on within her. Then she said, "You are—are . . ."

"Doc Savage," offered homely Monk, a pleased grin on his features. "And the longer you know him, the more he'll astonish you."

Lin Pretti looked at Doc.

"But how—how did you . . ."

"The use of makeup enabled me to do several things," the bronze man said dryly.

Lin Pretti flushed.

"Thank you," she said, "for saving my life when Lurgent tried to kill me."

"Why did he try to kill you?" Doc asked.

His query got silence.

"Was the story about a man—a vicious slayer—coming from the moon, true?" Doc inquired.

Silence again.

Doc got the truth serum. "I dislike doing this," he said.

They ran into a startling setback. Lin Pretti did not react to the truth serum!

Doc gave her as large a quantity as he dared—enough, in fact, to make several men talk profusely, and ordinary women too. But Lin Pretti became only a little dull, and did not talk. She mumbled incoherently, her words mixing into each other so that it was impossible to make out what she was saying. Doc didn't dare give her any more of the truth serum because a greater amount would be fatal.

Of all Doc's aides, Monk was the most astonished. He had made that batch of truth serum, under the direction of Doc. He set about immediately checking on it. He could find nothing wrong.

Not until Doc pricked her arm and Monk—he carried a portable chemical outfit wherever he went—made an analysis of the girl's arterial fluid did the truth come out: her system has been made immune to truth serum! Just as regular usage of many drugs can make the user comparatively immune, so had this girl evidently been made impervious to truth serums.

"But I can't understand such a thing!" attractive Pat gasped.

"Spies," Doc said quietly, "of many nations now receive immunization from truth serums as part of their training."

The bronze man did not elaborate on that statement.

The rest of the day they spent in an intensive search for some trace of Johnny. They found the dynamite intact at the trap which had been set for Doc. The bronze man set it off. The blast did demolish much of the hilltop.

The bronze man did not go near the house when he set off the blast, lest Lurgent or another be watching from a distance. As he had known the location of the hidden explosives, Doc had merely set it off with bullets from a high-powered rifle from a distance.

They did not find Johnny.

They did not find Lurgent.

And they did not find any trace of the Man on the Moon.

Late that afternoon, a large plane arrived from Doc's criminal-curing "college." The prisoners were loaded aboard, with the exception of Lin Pretti and unconscious, almost dying Vesterate. The attendants on the plane—surgeons skilled and trained by Doc Savage—aided in another operation to preserve Vesterate's life. Before they left—taking the crooks away to be "cured"—they expressed some doubt that Vesterate would live at all.

Doc made a circuit of the countryside in one of the planes from the meadow behind the farmhouse, and Renny did likewise in the other craft. They found nothing.

"That meeting place we got from one of the prisoners is our only hope," Renny grumbled glumly. "The Lurgent gang was to assemble at the Caribenna Steamship Co. pier in Norfolk, weren't they?"

"Early tomorrow morning," Doc agreed quietly.

Renny emitted a sudden yell. "Doc! Doc! We've overlooked something!"

"Yes?"

"That blue capsule this fellow from the moon—Vesterate —cut out of his leg!" Renny boomed. "We haven't examined it!"

"Behemoth examined it," Doc said dryly. "Here."

He produced the capsule from where he had taped it under his armpit, handed it to Renny.

The blue thing, they perceived, was of glass, and one end, once sealed with a blue glass-hard wax, had been opened by Doc.

Inside was a sheet of thin paper. Renny spread this out. It bore a design—a line drawing of geometric contour. It seemed to be a picture of a medallion, generally rectangular, with rounded corners and an upraised design.

The design: a half-moon with a tiny figure perched on one corner; the figure—a tiny devil, with horns and a long tail with a spike on the end. The devil held a pitchfork.

"Give me that!" Lin Pretti cried unexpectedly.

They looked at her, astonished.

"Give me that, and turn me loose, and your troubles will be over!" the girl gasped.

"Give us the story that goes with it," Doc directed.

She only stared at him, then said, "Please," plaintively.

"Our friend Johnny may be dead," Doc said. "We are not forgetting anything."

"But I had nothing to do with your friend getting captured," Lin Pretti said.

"We know that," the bronze man said. "However, you are deliberately holding out information that might enable us to rescue him, perhaps even catch the gang holding him prisoner."

"I—I can't tell you anything."

"You mean you won't, even though you could!" Monk snapped.

She fell silent. They could get no more out of her.

Monk finally fell to studying the drawing of the medallion.

"The Devil on the Moon," he muttered finally. "That's what I call a fine symbol for this mess."

Chapter IX

THE NORFOLK TRAIL

A mild fog enwrapped Old Point Comfort, Norfolk harbor and that tiny basin used by yachtsmen, The Hague, as Doc Savage brought one of his two planes down in the early morning darkness. Renny piloted the other plane, close behind. Doc had a Norfolk harbor chart tucked beside him. He had glanced at it earlier, and did not consult it afterward.

The planes were idling. They also carried unusually efficient silencers, which the bronze man had designed.

Doc Savage picked up the green lights on the drawbridge at the mouth of The Hague. He cleared them, fishtailed away speed, hit the water, vaulted, settled again, and the plane came to a halt. A moment later Renny had the other craft nearby.

Doc and Renny got down on the floats with ordinary canoe paddles and manipulated the planes into shallow water, where the light and efficient anchors were put overboard. They prepared to unload.

"You will stay here with Lin Pretti and Vesterate," Doc told Pat. "Chemistry and Habeas will remain too; I don't think it would be safe to bring them along with us."

Pat said indignantly, "Already you're discriminating against my sex. You know I can handle a gun as well as— well, I won't be ridiculous and say as well as you can. But I can shoot."

"Which is a bad thing itself," Doc said quietly.

The bronze man had one principle which was peculiar in view of his hazardous calling: he was insistent that neither he nor his men ever directly take a human life. Their enemies had perished on occasion, but through their own vicious scheming having backfired on them, never as a direct result of any of the bronze man's crowd deliberately slaying.

Pat Savage didn't argue. The truth was she considered herself rather lucky that Doc had permitted her to come at all. Vesterate's desperately critical condition influenced his decision, too. Pat knew something about nursing.

Doc Savage and his aides unloaded small metal cases of equipment from the plane. These were portable, and mostly contained Doc's scientific gadgets.

Little was said. They were worried about Johnny, their captured friend. Johnny was more to them than a noted archaeologist and geologist; he meant as much to them as any of their closest kin.

Doc and his aides headed for the Caribenna Steamship Co. pier.

It looked as if a giant had pushed against one side, straining the great timbers, giving the roof a swayback. Probably the giant had been the tail of some Hatteras storm. The weather had worked on it for years, peeling the paint, rusting the corrugated roof, loosening boards. The shape was that of a banana crate, with a gable roof. Once there had been a name across the front, but weather had erased that:

KEEP OUT!
By order of Caribenna SS receivers

This admonition on a sign outside the tall old board fence was the only identification. It was an abandoned pier and warehouse.

Doc Savage halted his men some distance away. He opened one of the equipment cases and took out two pieces of apparatus. The first was a tiny portable radio-telephone receiver-transmitter, not effective any great distance, but more compact than the average folding Kodak.

The second device was a highly sensitive "finder" of electromagnetic fields. It consisted of a pickup aerial, an amplifier of extremely high gain, and a headset. It was capable of picking a conversation off a telephone wire at a distance of scores of yards.

"Get under cover," Doc said. "We'll keep in touch with the radio." He picked up another equipment case to take along.

Doc's four aides took cover.

Doc vaulted into a vacant lot, merged with some weeds, and the murk of early dawn seemed to digest him. He appeared again, using his "finder" near the warehouse.

One type of modern burglar alarm is most difficult to defeat. Not photoelectric "eyes," which ring a bell when an invisible beam is intercepted. That beam can be located with proper filters. But buried wires, surrounded by a magnetic field which is upset by the intrusion of even a human body, are almost unlocatable—except with the device Doc was using.

The alarm wires were strung around the fence. He did not go near them, but moved to the right, circling widely, and reached the waterfront. He stripped to bathing trunks, of silk, which he wore in lieu of underclothing.

From the equipment box Doc took goggles and a pair of diving "lungs" which were simply nasal clips, mouthpiece, and a breath-purifying tank which strapped to the chest. To keep himself on the bottom more readily, he carried a large rock, and entered the water.

It was very cold, very black, under the surface. By holding the luminous dial of a wrist compass close to his goggles, and keeping track of his steps, Doc bore toward the pier. It extended, building and all, out into the water and was, apparently, as much a boathouse as a pier.

He came up close to the end of the pier.

It was much lighter now. He could observe distinctly the outlines of two motor boats, rather large and ugly craft equipped with cabins. A type of boat called a "subchaser" during the Great War, and long outmoded.

MARINE FOOD SUPPLIES

This legend was freshly painted on each of the craft.

Three men with rifles were at the end of the pier, alertly watching, and listening to the silent burglar alarm.

A little later Doc Savage was aboard one of the boats. The bronze man was a master of stealth.

In the cabin of the craft was a heap of neat white duck

pants and equally neat white coats, and many white canvas aprons which bore the legend, "Marine Food Supplies, Norfolk, Virginia."

Doc waited.

When men began to arrive, they came furtively. Each of them was examined, had his face scrubbed with a bit of chemical, evidently to make sure he was not one of Doc Savage's aides, wearing makeup. They were the men Lurgent had hired. The ex-navy men. None of these men seemed to be native-born Americans, or had served in the U.S. Navy.

They were herded together. It was plain they had not yet been told what they were to do.

Lurgent came finally. He had a bodyguard, and did not look as if he had slept. He was still a vicious hawk of a man, but also an uneasy one.

"You birds get out of sight," he directed. "There's a tool shed over here."

The men went into the tool shed.

Lurgent and the three guards were left in view. "Any sign of Doc Savage?" Lurgent asked.

They said there hadn't been. Said it as if much relieved.

"What're we waiting for?" one asked.

"Help me with this," Lurgent grunted, instead of answering.

Lurgent and his men then set up a small portable radio transmitter and receiver. This had a loudspeaker, and a small velocity microphone on a stand. Lurgent and the others waited about twenty minutes.

A large limousine arrived. It had a uniformed driver, the rear was curtained, and each door bore a coat of arms. The machine had diplomatic license plates.

A large, rather pompous man alighted. He had a heavy jaw, dark, determined eyes, and an upstanding shock of gray hair.

Doc Savage, watching covertly from the boat—he was taking advantage of an open porthole—recognized the newcomer instantly.

The new arrival's face had been in the newspapers many times, both in America and Europe. He was a diplomat; more correctly, an ambassador of a European nation to Washington.

This ambassador's country had been one of the leading

menaces to European peace. The government, not many months before, had declared unprovoked war on a smaller country. The world knew that the sole purpose of this violent act was conquest, territorial expansion.

Other European powers had resented the conquest. The League of Nations had taken a stand. The situation had grown tense. One European power had rushed its battle fleet into the aggressive government's waters. War had seemed imminent.

Then a surprising thing had happened. The nation about to declare war on the conquesting government had colonies abroad. These colonies had hitherto been fairly peaceful. But suddenly, violent riots and outbreaks occurred. The colonies had all but revolted. The country had been kept so busy with its own troubles that it had permitted the other power to go ahead with a cruel conquest which had resulted in thousands of deaths.

This ambassador was that iron-fisted ruler's representative in Washington. He stared at Lurgent.

"So you are the Man on the Moon," he said.

Lurgent shrugged his hard shoulders. "Your Highness is mistaken."

The ambassador did not speak good English, as he snapped, "But it was your voice which called me in Washington and told me the Man on the Moon desired to confer with me here."

"Right," Lurgent grunted. "But the conferring is going to take place over that radio." He pointed at the radio-telephone he had set up.

"Yes." The ambassador scowled. "But we will be overheard. Radio is a public medium . . ."

"There is a scrambler on that set, Your Highness," Lurgent said shortly. "No one will understand you."

Lurgent walked over to the radio and switched it into operation.

Doc Savage hurriedly clicked his own tiny radio on—it was waterproof, and he had fastened it to the breath-purifier of his diving lungs—and got in touch with his aides. They were, they said, hidden in someone's chicken house about half a mile distant.

A very dirty chicken house, complained the fastidious Ham, who did the talking. Doc, whispering into the sensitive midget mike, directed them to get their sets onto loop aerials and make them directional; the equipment was designed so it could be made into radio direction-finding efficiency by merely moving switches.

"Get two bearings, if possible, on the other end of this radio-telephone conversation," stated Doc. "It is going through a scrambler, so you won't be able to understand it, but you may get bearings by which we can locate the other transmitter."

The ambassador had been looking at Lurgent's radio doubtfully. Now Lurgent stepped to it, said, "Here's His Highness," then stepped back and looked at the visitor. "Go ahead."

"Ah—ah—hello!" the ambassador said tentatively.

A voice disguised as if the speaker were holding something between his teeth started speaking. The owner did not waste time, but said; "Some months ago, your nation was grabbing another small country. Another nation was about to put a stop to the hogging, and your government hired me to start riots and a little revolt in the nation's colonies. That is my business.

"For my work, the price was twenty million and some odd dollars. Your government agreed to that. I did the job. And now your country is welshing. I will not have that!"

The ambassador's eyes snapped.

"I fail to see what you can do about it," he said coldly. "The price we will pay is five millions. We will pay it in the bonds of my country."

"Your Highness, the bonds of your country aren't worth half-par value outside your boundary," said the Man on the Moon. "I want cash. Not five—twenty!"

"There will be no compromise."

"That the final word?"

"It is."

The Man on the Moon said hollowly, "Your Highness, may I remind you that you are double-crossing the most remarkable organization ever assembled? I kept your ruler from being put in his place a few months ago. I can smash him just as easily as I did that."

"We do not fear you."

"You had better. For months you have been trying with your secret agents to get a line on me. They have failed."

"You are wasting time . . ."

"Let me finish," said the Man on the Moon. "Let me remind you about one of your nation's secret agents—Tony Vesterate by name. He disappeared, you recall? Would you care to know my men got him and took him to the moon? True, he later escaped, but I do not think he is now alive. He tried to reach another of your agents here in America—a girl named Lin Pretti, who had her headquarters at the roadhouse known as the Spanish Plantation."

Doc Savage's regular, metallic-looking features did not change expression at this. But the information must have clarified the mystery greatly—Vesterate, a foreign spy who had escaped; Lin Pretti a fellow spy whom he was trying to reach for safety. And Lurgent had been trying to wipe out these two spies. But even this left much unexplained. What manner of skycraft had Vesterate arrived in? What was the significance of the medallion sketch which Vesterate had carried? And, incredible as it seemed, could the prisoner have been taken to the moon?

"There is no need of talking further!" the ambassador snapped.

"Perhaps," said the Man on the Moon, "I will have to threaten you."

The ambassador snarled into the microphone, "My master racketeer, I am empowered to tell you at this point that all negotiations are off! From now hence, you can, as the Americans say, whistle for your money!"

He walked out.

There came into being within the old pier house a strange, subdued trilling, an eerie sound that might have been made by a breeze trickling through a denuded jungle. It was the sound of Doc Savage, the small strange note which he made unconsciously in moments of intense mental activity. Just now, it meant that Doc Savage was comprehending the nature of activity engaged in by this sinister one who called himself the Man on the Moon.

The Man on the Moon had taken the practices of disreputable private detective agencies and enlarged them to international scope. Crooked private detectives in America hired out to break strikes, to beat up individuals, to frame innocent victims with crimes. This, then, seemed to be what the Man on the Moon did to nations. It was a workable scheme, but astounding in its proportions. It caused Doc Savage's small sound. He realized he was making it, and quickly silenced it.

No one had heard.

Lurgent called loudly into the microphone, "He turned us down. Shall we go ahead?"

"Proceed!" The Man on the Moon swore violently. "By tomorrow, our welshing friend will have a war on his hands that will cost him twenty billion, not twenty million!"

"Right."

Lurgent walked into the tool shed where he had ordered his hired crook-sailors. He began talking to them. Doc Savage listened intently, but the hollow acoustics of the place, and the distance, as well as the low voice Lurgent was using, defeated even his trained hearing.

The bronze man could get no idea of what was said.

Lurgent's men filed out. The agility with which they formed a long line showed their naval training. Lurgent, standing in front of them, scowled down the line.

"You've had a minute to think it over," he said. "There's plenty of money in it. Do any of you want to back out? Does it scare any of you?"

There was a moment of silence, then one man stepped forward. He looked scared.

"I didn't figure anything as big as this," he gulped nervously. "I—uh—I quit."

Lurgent grinned at him. "That's all right, buddy. No harm done." He smiled pleasantly at the others. "Anybody else? I wouldn't blame you for quitting."

Another man hesitated, then stepped out. "Me, too." He was pale, frightened.

Lurgent laughed easily. "Any others?"

There were no others.

Lurgent drew two of his long-barreled silenced single-shot pistols and shot each of the two quitters through the brain.

Chapter X

THE FISH STEALERS

There ensued a moment of horror when even the ex-sailors were aghast, although Lurgent had obviously picked them for their hard unscrupulousness as well as their naval experience. More than one pale face was in the line. The little speech which Lurgent now made, stating that he expected military obedience and any man who shirked or hesitated would be shot, did not cheer them greatly.

Lurgent then stated that he had shot the two quitters simply because no information about this project could be permitted to leak out.

He finished by offering a reward of fifty thousand dollars in cash to any man who could manage to kill the bronze man, Doc Savage.

The men now got aboard the boats. Lurgent must have instructed them what to do while they were in the tool shed. They began putting on the white suits and the aprons which marked them as simple marine grocery deliverymen.

Doc Savage had crept forward and crouched in the anchor-cable locker. It was unlikely they would look there. The men were too much on edge to roam around looking at the craft.

"Cast off!" Lurgent ordered. "And all of you have guns ready."

The hawseholes into the anchor-cable locker opened on either side of the bow. Doc, watching through them, saw the decrepit pier house recede in the swirling early morning fog.

The second boat was accompanying them, also loaded with Lurgent's men.

Doc put his tiny radio into use.

"Did you locate the source of the second station using that scrambler?" he asked.

Ham said, "Well, we got a couple of bearings. Any sign of Johnny, Doc?"

"No mention of Johnny," the bronze man said grimly. "Get those bearings down on paper."

"Sure. Shall we try to find the transmitting station?"

"Do exactly that," the bronze man said. "And be careful. The fellow who spoke over that station was the Man on the Moon."

"Good!" Ham growled. "We're getting closer to him. But say, how about you?"

"Don't worry about me," Doc directed.

"Right," Ham said.

That ended the radio conversation, and Doc remained quiet while the two fake grocery delivery boats ploughed through the fog. The craft seemed to have a definite destination.

The submarine was very large, very bright, very new. It was almost three hundred feet long, wonderfully streamlined. Four deck guns—themselves waterproof—crouched in iron warts along the deck. There were big hatches which could open, and a catapult with a scouting plane already in place for launching would rise by machinery.

From flagstaffs fluttered great flags. The flags belonged to the nation ruled by the iron-fisted ruler who had been discussed by the ambassador and the Man on the Moon.

The sub was moored to a deserted concrete dock not far from the U. S. navy yard.

The two boats containing Lurgent's men pulled alongside, threw lines and made fast. They began shouldering baskets of groceries—these had been on the second craft.

They were challenged when they started to get aboard the submarine. The U-boat crew explained their craft was closed to visitors.

The submarine's officer did not add that his government had sent this craft across the Atlantic just to show how modern a navy it had. But that had been in the newspapers.

Lurgent did some lying. He was glib. He said the sub commander had ordered groceries, and they were delivering them. The officer snapped that the commander was below, asleep. There was palaver. But Lurgent's men got aboard.

They descended into the submarine.

Lurgent's men ambled through the sub. In a moment they had scattered to strategic points. Yanking the top layer of groceries out of their baskets, they uncovered stubby, somewhat clumsy-looking automatic pistols of a foreign make which, when fitted with oversize magazines shaped like snails, became literally machine-pistols. They began menacing the crew. Most of the U-boat personnel were asleep forward, where they were locked up.

Brazen and simply, within five minutes, Lurgent had taken the submarine, the newest and finest, which the foreign power had sent junketing to show how militaristic it was.

Lurgent assembled some of his men in the control room, just below the main hatch.

"Radio operator," he said.

"Yes, sir," said one of the men.

"Here is a radio message!" Lurgent snapped. "Read it out loud."

The man read. The message simply stated that the government was declaring war herewith on one of the largest European nations. A nation which, incidentally, was the same one which had nearly prevented the conquest, and would have, had it not been for the colonial troubles which the Man on the Moon had apparently created for pay. Pay which he hadn't received. Feeling between these two powers was still none too sociable.

Doc Savage, on deck and beside the control-room hatch, could hear each word of the war declaration.

Lurgent said, "I had that read so you fellows will know what we're really doing. It's time you knew now."

He paused for effect.

"At anchor near here is a warship belonging to this other nation. Aboard the warship is the admiral of their navy. He is here on a goodwill visit, sent to counteract the publicity the government hoped to get when it sent this submarine."

His voice hardened.

"We cast off from this dock. You are submarine men and can handle this craft. That's why I hired all ex-submarine men. We line our torpedo tubes up on that warship. We send that declaration of war. Then we torpedo the warship, and escape out to sea. No one but the ruler will know it wasn't a genuine declaration of war and a bold stroke to get their admiral."

He waited, then laughed grimly.

"Europe is ripe. There is no doubt but that an incident like this will pull the trigger." Lurgent cursed viciously. "That damn country will get whipped. We'll teach it to welsh out of paying our organization. Any questions?"

There were no questions.

"Get to your stations!"

Doc Savage swung silently back to the two old fake grocery delivery boats. He dropped into one, tore the gasoline lines loose in the engine room, got matches out of the galley and set the leaking gasoline afire. It instantly made a big fire. He got the second boat flaming. The craft bloomed smoke.

The smoke would attract help.

Doc leaped to the control-room hatch. A man was coming up. Doc put a bronze hand on his face, shoved. The man fell. Doc dropped after him.

Lurgent cursed. He and two others were in the control room. They dug for guns. The man Doc had shoved howled in agony. He had broken something.

"Savage!" Lurgent squalled.

He hadn't recognized Doc at first, it seemed. Now he did, and he played safe.

"Get him!" he roared.

Then he leaped backward through a bulkhead door, vanishing.

The other two men hit Doc. There was nothing they could do but fight. They came in, still pulling their guns.

One man got his gun out, but never fired it because something got hold of his arm and twisted, and he looked down just in time to see that the bronze man's hand was gripping him, then he was blinded with an explosion of agony as the arm came out of joint.

The second man shot. He had not aimed carefully. The bullet missed. Doc, coming in, lashed out a long arm, knocked the gun aside.

The gun banged again. Doc's metallic hand slid down the arm to the gun hand. It seemed that he put no great pressure on the hand; he did not grimace, exhibit his teeth and strain his breathing as do most strong men while being strong. But the victim screamed terribly; the ends of his fingers bulged like stepped-on wieners under the pressure, and one fingertip split and emptied crimson.

Doc then took hold of the man's neck. He twisted, kneaded, doing something with his fingers—working almost as a chiropractor works. The man became limp, weirdly paralyzed from head to foot, but he kept his eyes open.

"It's the U. S. Navy!" Doc yelled, changing his voice.

It wouldn't hurt to scare Lurgent and the rest. As a matter of fact, Doc Savage did hold a rather high honorary commission in the navy.

Shouts rang through the submarine as Lurgent's men made known to each other that the man of bronze was aboard. Lurgent shrieked for them to charge the control room.

Doc flung to the controls. The craft could be operated from the master wheels and gauges here. He made adjustments quickly, violently—started the bow tanks filling, blowing the stern tanks completely at the same time. His idea was to stand the submersible on her nose to make it difficult for the gang to move.

They defeated him.

They did it by disconnecting the controls fore and aft. The sub, of course, was equipped with manual local station controls. The craft remained level.

Doc got one of the guns of the men he had felled, fired into the steel corridor beyond the bulkhead, not trying to shoot any one, but driving lead into the floor matting. The metal passage whooped with replying shots. All of them came from aft. That was what he had wanted to know.

He waited, then shoved head and gun out silently. The weapon whacked twice; a man yelled as his pistol left mangled fingers; a second man turned around and around, holding his perforated shoulder and bawling at the top of his voice.

Only those two had been showing themselves. Doc lunged out into the corridor, sped aft. He was taking a chance. If an enemy shoved a gun into view, he had to hit the gun or the hand holding it before the weapon could be aimed and fired. And the light was none too good.

Then one of the men tossed a steaming tear-gas grenade

into the passage. Doc had no mask, no protection for his eyes. He was driven back. A gun whacked behind him.

A compartment door gaped near, and Doc went in there. His flake-gold eyes roved, distinguished no other exit—only two comfortable berths, a desk. Officers' quarters, evidently.

Doc slammed the door, waited for the tear gas to penetrate down the corridor. Somewhere forward, machinery began grinding. It was about the noise a power drawbridge makes when opening. Doc recognized it—the plane catapult lifting out of its recess!

Lurgent! Preparing to escape!

There couldn't be another reason for getting the plane ready to catapult. Doc opened the door. The gun smashed again; its lead hit the edge of the door. The gunner must have been wearing a gas mask. Doc jerked back, banged the door shut. Already, the tear gas had made his eyes moisten a little. The passage was full of the stuff.

Two ordinary drinking glasses stood in a locker over the cabin desk. Doc got one of the glasses, jammed the edge against his bronze skin, over his right eye, hard enough to make an airtight joint. This protected one eye from the tear gas, for he could see, even if in a distorted fashion, through the bottom of the glass. He shut his other eye, held his breath, went out into the passage, shot twice and brought the gunner down with a broken leg, and raced back to the control room.

En route, Doc heard a sound as if someone had coughed and dropped iron on iron at the same time.

Reaching the deck, he saw the submarine scouting plane, a tiny and fast craft, moaning away. Lurgent was reared up in the cockpit, looking back. He ducked down. Doc fired a gun, but got no result; this type of plane had a lightly armored cockpit to protect the flier.

Lurgent banked and came back. Cowl machine guns on his craft cackled and stung at the sub. Smoke gushing from the burning boats made marksmanship difficult. Anyway, Doc was below, dogging the control-room doors shut to keep the men within the submersible.

Banking up, plane motor baying, Lurgent came back. This time his machine guns cackled only briefly. Passing overhead, he detached a bomb. It missed, but not enough. There was a roar, convulsion, a wave of harbor water which flooded the decks and sloshed down the hatches.

The sub rolled. Plates split. Water, gurgling and roaring, sheeting over gratings, sloshing walls. Then screams of men afraid of death followed.

Lurgent roared away in the plane.

Doc undogged the control-room doors to let the men out. Then he whipped on deck, leaped ashore and lost himself among tall weeds and ramshackle waterfront buildings.

The bronze man did not remain in the neighborhood.

Within a short time, fire apparatus, police and a squad of marines arrived from the nearby navy yard. There was a great deal of uproar, shouting, rescuing of people, and the submarine sank in shallow water where it could easily be raised again. Explanations followed, then the arresting of ex-sailors turned pirates; but fully half of Lurgent's hirelings escaped.

Chapter XI

THE MERCHANT OF DEATH

There was little doubt but that Doc Savage, by remaining behind and making explanations, could have cleared up a bit of confusion. A large bit, in fact. Neither the authorities nor the newspaper reporters, who arrived at the sunken submarine scene promptly, were at first willing to believe what they were told. Lurgent's men—those who hadn't drowned—did this telling.

It did sound fantastic that a mysterious international strong-arm organization headed by a name as ridiculous as the Man on the Moon could have been trying to steal a country's submarine in order to fake a declaration of war and sink another nation's battleship carrying an admiral—all to start a European war.

Nobody really swallowed the yarn for a while. Lurgent's gang, learning he had sunk the sub, talked freely, insisting the whole affair was a vengeance move of the Man on the Moon, who had not been paid for preventing a nation which had intended to stop a country's conquest.

Then someone mentioned Doc Savage. Presto! The thing immediately seemed less incredible. A wild search promptly began for Doc Savage. Newspapermen wanted to question him, and incidentally to smear his picture over the front pages.

This, it happened, was the principal reason Doc Savage had not remained. The bronze man did not like publicity. Not only did he dislike it, but it was dangerous—enabled too many enemies to know too much about him. He always did everything possible to escape a newspaperman.

Doc arrived back where he had left his clothing near the old Caribenna Steamship Co. pier. He had picked up a taxi-cab, the driver of which wondered mightily at a passenger who wore silk bathing trunks.

Paying the man with money from his clothing, Doc dressed inside the moving hack, then leaned back and spoke into the tiny radio.

"Ham!" he said, then said "Ham!" several times again before the voice of the dapper cane-carrying lawyer answered.

"By Jove, what happened?" Ham demanded anxiously. "We have been trying for half an hour to raise you."

"A little excitement," Doc explained quietly. The chaotic events of the last hour would reasonably have justified a bit of excitement. Unconcern was almost unnatural under the circumstances. Yet he'd said, "A little excitement."

This understatement, the calmness as well, was typical of the bronze man's control.

"Anything come of those radio-directional bearings on the Man on the Moon's radio transmitter?" Doc asked.

Ham said, "You'd better get over here, Doc. We've uncovered something interesting."

"Where are you?"

"That yacht basin—The Hague. Where we left the planes."

"I'll be there in a few minutes," Doc said. That ended the conversation.

The Hague lies almost on the edge of the Norfolk business section. It is deep along one side, shallow along the other, walled around with concrete. It is frequently used by naval gigs which call there for officers, throwing wakes which aggravate the yachtsmen who also anchor there, or moor their craft to the docks. The yachtsmen are usually swearing at the naval gigs.

A gig had just passed, and Doc Savage's two planes were rocking in the wake as the bronze man alighted on shore and dismissed his bewildered taxi driver.

Pat, standing on one plane wing, was giving the gig sailors a piece of her mind, informing them she had a desperately ill man aboard and didn't want him shaken up.

"Pat!" Doc called, his trained voice as nearly anxious as it ever became. "Are the others here?"

Pat pointed across The Hague. "They're over there on that yacht."

It was not a small yacht—over a hundred feet. She was white, two-masted, schooner-rigged. Exhaust outlets indicated she was also powered.

"When did that craft put in here?" Doc queried.

"Half an hour ago."

Doc walked around The Hague, passed to the rear of several small shipyards catering to yachtsmen, stepped across a wharf that was greasy and strewn with timbers, rope ends and old fenders, and mounted a mahogany gangplank which was floored with white rubber matting.

When he stepped on deck, two sailors got in front of him, holding big army automatics.

One began, "All right, who—" He stopped, opened his mouth wide. "Doc Savage!" he gasped. "Ah—your men are waiting below!"

The sailors put their guns away. Doc paused for a moment, buttoning his vest. He had unbuttoned it en route to the schooner for this very purpose. Fastening it now gave him time to survey the scene, seeking visual answer to the possible question—was it a trap?

When big-fisted Renny, the engineer, appeared, the question answered itself.

Renny came quickly to Doc and began rumbling, trying to make his great voice low, but not succeeding very well. "This hooker—but say! Doc, did you find Johnny?"

The bronze man shook his head slowly, grimly. "No trace." Then; "Why are you aboard here?"

"This hooker came in here half an hour or so ago," Renny explained. "One of the sailors aboard must have recognized Pat. Anyway, the owner called over to her. He wanted to see you. Was on his way to New York to see you, he claimed. So Pat told us—and here we are."

"What does the owner want?"

"He can tell you. He's below here. It's kind of nutty."

The yacht owner said, "My name is Aldace K. O'Hannigan."

He was a big red man who looked as if he had been lightly boiled, then spattered with brown ink. He had very dark freckles. His height almost equalled that of Doc Savage. His hair was a flaming red, and every hair stood straight up.

He looked Doc Savage levelly up and down, came forward firmly and almost as if trying to domineer, and put out his hand. Doc took the hand. The other man's sinews in the red-freckled wrist stood out as he tried a crushing grip.

Doc did not change expression.

Aldace K. O'Hannigan took his hand back, looked at it, moved the fingers as if he thought something had happened to them. He put the hand in his pocket quickly. A faint film of sweat had come out on his forehead.

"Sure, and be dogged if I'll try to outgrip *you* again," he said.

He had a rather high voice which somehow led to the expectation that he would any minute burst out singing "Mother Machree."

"Know me?" he asked. "Your lads here didn't."

"Munitions dealer," Doc Savage said quietly. "American citizen, but noted for sales of used planes, arms and ammunition in the Chinese, Ethiopian and Spanish troubles of recent years. Congress of the United States recently investigated your activities in selling war munitions to belligerent foreign nations."

"Sure, and it's a merchant of death, they called me." Big Aldace K. O'Hannigan popped his knee with a red-freckled palm and laughed. "But divil of a memory ye've got at that."

Doc Savage, who did not approve of war nor munitions manufacturers or sellers, said, "We have not yet taken the trouble to investigate you closely. What did you want to see me about?"

Aldace K. O'Hannigan gave his leather belt a hitch, swiped one hand across his mouth—and half closed an eye at Doc Savage.

"Bedad, and so ye don't like me. I'm a-seeing that, never mind. But I'm going right ahead and tell ye I'm after needing a stout lad with your reputation to help me out of a jam."

Doc said shortly, "Our services are not for hire."

This was true. The bronze man possessed a source of fabulous wealth in a remote Central American valley, from which he summoned, occasionally, such quantities of gold as he needed in his gigantic operations, as well as in many charity projects of which he was the benefactor.

"I know ye don't, and begorra it's divil a bit of sense I think it shows that ye don't. Which, sor, is neither here nor the other place. I'm after hearing ye make a business of helping people out of their troubles, an' sure it's troubles this O'Hannigan has got."

"You, in trouble?" Doc asked quietly.

"Och! Up to me two dirty ears."

"Want to tell us about it?" Doc asked.

"Bedad, and I do that."

He proceeded to do so, but as a preliminary move, he fished inside a vest pocket—he wore a gaudily checked tweed suit—and brought out a small metal object. He passed this to Doc.

It was a medallion, somewhat near two inches across, the same in width, the corners slightly rounded. There was an upraised design: a depiction of a quarter-moon, with a figure seated on one corner. The figure was that of a devil with a long, pronged tail and a pair of jauntily curving horns. A hilarious-looking devil.

"Faith, and I'm wonderin' if ye find anythin' to tweak your interest in that doojigger," said O'Hannigan.

Doc did. It was the medallion pictured in the drawing which the mysterious green man of the rocket, Tony Vesterate, had carried in his own flesh. Doc's interest was well tweaked.

"Where did you get it, O'Hannigan?"

"Where? Sure, and 'twas given me by a very nice boy indeed who is me friend."

"His name?"

"Bob Thomas."

Doc Savage's flake-gold eyes moved briefly over his four aides—Long Tom, Renny, Monk and Ham, the latter two still with their two strange pets, Habeas Corpus and Chemistry. It was quite plain now why the four had come aboard this big yacht, and also why they had summoned the bronze man.

"I wear it on me watch chain as a normal thing," said Aldace K. O'Hannigan.

"Bob Thomas gave it to you?"

"Yes, sor. 'Twas one of two of thim just alike that the boy had."

"Why should Bob Thomas give it to you?"

"Well, man, and why shouldn't he? A divil a big life insurance policy I bought of the boy, and he wanted to show his appreciation, would be my guess. 'Tis a gold medal, but it was also a nice bit of clinking coin that Bob Thomas got as commission."

"Bob Thomas had two medallions just alike, and that is one of them?" Doc repeated slowly.

" 'Tis what I said, no less."

Doc Savage's four aides, watching their bronze chief, got no inkling of what was on his mind from his expression. But they knew it was probably that he was reviewing his career as Behemoth.

"What is your trouble?" Doc queried.

"Well, sor, a little snip of a man come to me two weeks ago and wanted to buy the medallion. Faith, and why should I sell? I'd took a fancy to it, and it was a gift; and no true son of woman sells a friend's gift. Och! Ye know what? That snip offered me twenty thousand of Uncle Sammy's good dollars for this medal jigger! Then he got tough, and I got tough, and bedad, he got me foot in the natural place and went out on his blitherin' ear.

"Since then, they've been tryin' to kill and rob me, no less. Divil a moment of peace I've had, what with knives and prowlers and even a wee spot of poison in me breakfast oatmeal, the same bein' discovered by the poor cat which jumped on the table when me back was turned and sampled the dish."

The homely Monk put into the recital, saying in his small voice, "As I understand it, you got scared and were on your way to Doc . . ."

" 'Tis scared of no man that I be!" O'Hannigan roared, purpling.

"All right, all right, don't yell at me," Monk grunted.

"Divil well will I yell at anybody it pleases me to yell at!"

"I see," Monk said, "you're going to be a sociable cuss to get along with."

Doc Savage's trained voice—it seemed to carry, when he so desired, an almost hypnotic power to calm others—quieted the incipient disturbance. Aldace K. O'Hannigan admitted he had been worried and on his way to see Doc, of whom he had heard. He had thought the mystery of this would appeal to the bronze man, as it would have.

But little more in details was brought out by the discussion. The attacks might have been perpetrated by someone aboard the yacht, but probably not, because they had all occurred while the craft was in some port.

Doc and his four aides retired to a secluded part of the deck and talked it over. Doc made sure they were behind a lifeboat so lip readers would be defeated.

"Where did the radio-compass bearings on the Man on the Moon's radio transmitter take you?" Doc asked.

"No dice," said Renny.

"What?"

"The harbor. Right out in the channel. There wasn't any sign of a boat there, of course, when we arrived. We asked around, but that fog this morning—well, nobody knew just what had gone up and down the harbor."

Big-fisted Renny put his tremendous hands on his hips and squinted at Doc Savage.

"We've been wondering," he added.

"About this schooner just happening into The Hague?" Doc queried.

"Sure. Holy cow! This hooker might have been out in the harbor about where the Man on the Moon's radio transmitter was. And there's radio aboard here. Whether there's a scrambler aboard or not, we don't know. We haven't seached. But if there is one aboard we'll . . ."

"We will search," Doc said.

They found Aldace K. O'Hannigan, and told him they would, if he didn't mind, look the boat and his crew over closely for anything suspicious.

"Bedad, go ahead," said O'Hannigan.

They knew then they would not find anything.

They didn't.

O'Hannigan confronted them. "Sure now, and look. 'Tis a favor I'm askin' ye, and if ye do it, I'll give a reasonable sum to charity, 'though will doubtless break me dirty heart to do so."

"What is the favor?" Doc asked calmly.

"Will ye be lettin' me go with ye from now hence until this blitherin' mystery is solved?"

"Of course," Doc agreed readily. "We'll be glad to have you with us."

Which surprised the bronze man's aides no little, until he privately explained to them that while O'Hannigan's story of Bob Thomas giving him the medallion, then someone trying to get it, was possibly true, nonetheless it did seem a bit pat and coincidental. What with one thing and another, it was just as well they had red, freckled munitions-seller O'Hannigan with them and kept an eye on him.

"I'm itching to lick that son of a gun," said Long Tom, the electrical wizard, unexpectedly.

Long Tom was usually a peaceful soul. And since he did not look capable of licking a twelve-year-old boy, his statement seemed slightly grotesque.

Chapter XII

BACK OF THE EIGHT BALL

Later in the morning, Doc Savage assigned each of his men a unit part in a general search for some trace of Johnny, Lurgent or the Man on the Moon. They scattered to this task.

Doc Savage himself visited the navy yard police jail—it wasn't called exactly that, but this was what it amounted to —and was in conference with officials. Not only the navy yard commandant was there, but important U. S. government officials had arrived, for this business of sinking a submarine belonging to a foreign power was serious business. No one ever knew what this frenzied nation might do; it might even declare war on the United States.

Doc Savage told the story, leaving out no truths. He was heard in amazement.

Even the espionage department of the U. S. government— there wasn't supposed to be a United States spy system, of course—knew nothing about the Man on the Moon's giant strong-arm organization which rented out its services.

Doc Savage then gave some advice, which was hurriedly acted upon. Undercover men and all other agencies were put to work immediately to try to trace the Man on the Moon's organization. Men were held in reserve to rush to any spot on the slightest signal.

There was a great deal of excitement, but despite it all, the bronze man remained calm. He voiced opinions and even helped in some of the preparations. Some of the officials even went so far as to order that the bronze man should be closely guarded. It was with difficulty that Doc Savage talked them out of an armed bodyguard. He explained that he and his men worked better alone, and they could accomplish more if they worked in secrecy rather than give their plans away by letting everyone know what they were up to.

After the conference, Doc was permitted to question the captured Lurgent thugs. From each of them, he demanded to know if Johnny was alive, and if he was, where he could be found.

The former Lurgent gang seemed to think Johnny was still alive. And if he was, he was in the company of the Man on the Moon, the men thought. Naturally, they did not know the whereabouts of the Man on the Moon.

Doc did not return to the plane at once. He found a swarm of newspaper reporters. Somehow they had learned Doc was owner of the two craft in The Hague. Doc observed them from a distance, did not show himself, and went to a telephone and called the navy yard. Shortly a half-dozen naval gigs arrived and kept newspapermen and photographers at a distance.

Doc returned to the two planes, determined to leave the spot as soon as his four aides reported on their search. He advised Pat as much.

Pat Savage, who had seen no action so far, thought the whole affair rather slow. Playing the part of nurse to the barely living Tony Vesterate had depressed her, as well.

Lin Pretti occupied one of the plane seats listlessly. She was handcuffed to a bracket which supported the seat.

Doc told Lin Pretti, "You should talk freely to us."

She stared at him. "I do not dare."

"We have only to turn you over to the government," Doc said. "And you will get at least ten years in a Federal penitentiary. If it was in wartime, you would be shot."

She gasped. "What—why—what makes you think . . ."

"Because you are a spy." Doc named the nation she was a spy for.

The slow paling of the attractive young woman's face was final proof that she was an espionage agent.

Doc let her think it over for a while, which was a wise move, because before long she began to talk. She admitted she was a secret agent of the foreign power, in America and headquartered near the Spanish Plantation roadhouse because it happened to be near Washington. Her work was merely to keep her eyes open, question military officials whom she vamped with her good looks, and pick up any other bits of information that might come from other sources.

She could not give much further information on the Man on the Moon. There was such an individual. For many months the government had been trying to find out who he was. Tony Vesterate, one of the nation's secret agents, had been assigned to the Man on the Moon work and had disappeared.

Lin Pretti admitted she had lied about men coming from the moon and murdering people in her country. That story had been merely to deceive Behemoth.

"Do you think Tony Vesterate was taken to the moon?" Doc asked.

The girl closed her eyes and shuddered. "Yes—yes, I do believe that."

"Why?"

"There have been stories—rumors—of prisoners taken to the moon by the Man on the Moon," the girl explained.

"Where was Tony Vesterate seized?" Doc asked.

"In what country, you mean?"

"Yes."

"Here in the United States," Lin Pretti replied.

Doc Savage's strange, small, trilling sound was faintly audible after that, indicating that Tony Vesterate being seized in the United States surprised him.

He was silent for a while.

"Why did you say the drawing of that medallion would clear all this up?" Doc asked.

The girl showed puzzlement. "What do you mean?"

"The medallion sketch," Doc repeated. "The sketch that was in the blue capsule Vesterate had in his flesh."

"Oh!" Her eyes flew wide. "Was that all it was? Why—I —don't understand! When I found Tony Vesterate, he gave me that capsule and from what he said, I thought it contained the name of the Man on the Moon."

"That capsule—the Man on the Moon—" Doc let that trail off thoughtfully.

Long Tom and Renny returned after a time. They had found no trace of Johnny, Lurgent, or the Man on the Moon. Like results were reported by Monk and Ham, who came back later. They added that the town was swarming with reporters and cameramen, and more were arriving.

It became plain that they could do no more toward conducting a secret search.

"We're leaving for New York," Doc Savage told everyone.

This news got into the hands of the reporters.

The bronze man's two planes took off. Immediately, a fleet of four newsreel planes—the craft had been buzzing around The Hague—fell in behind Doc's ships.

Doc Savage indicated clouds massed along the coast, angled over, and disappeared into them. Renny, flying close behind, followed. They kept in contact by radio, flew south instead of north, and lost the newsreel craft.

"Now," Doc said, "fly back and let me down near Norfolk. My plan is to stay there alone and investigate. The rest of you will go on to New York."

There was some objection to this. The four aides felt they were deserting a section where unfortunate Johnny might be held.

"The arrival of you four in New York will make it seem we have all gone back there," Doc explained. "You will take pains to make it appear I am with you. That will give me a chance to work alone here."

"Bedad, it sounds like a divil of a good idea, no less," said O'Hannigan, who was in one of the planes.

So they landed Doc Savage near Norfolk, where no one saw them.

The last they saw of the bronze man he was a tiny, remarkably proportioned figure which lifted an arm briefly at them as the planes climbed up into the sky.

Doc's four aides, Lin Pretti, O'Hannigan and Tony Vesterate landed on the Hudson River, opposite Manhattan Island, at dusk. More newspaper planes, or they might have been newsreel craft, had picked them up and followed them, even landing on the river.

Renny and Long Tom—Long Tom had taken Doc's place at the controls of one craft—taxied toward a large warehouse on the river front. This was a huge, substantial building—Doc's waterfront plane hangar and boathouse.

Long Tom caused the great doors to open by manipulating

a radio combination on a certain wave length—simply the principle by which telegraphers call their relay offices, but applied to radio and a mechanical door opener. The aides taxied the two planes inside and shut the doors on the nosy newsmen.

No one could have told that Doc was not aboard.

Eventually the party arrived, unobserved, at Doc Savage's headquarters on the eighty-sixth floor of one of the city's most impressive skyscrapers.

Not many people in the metropolis knew for a certainty that this aerie was still Doc's retreat. Of late, Doc had been carefully encouraging an impression he no longer could be found there. The skyscraper floors had even been renumbered, omitting the number thirteen, a common practice in hotels, so that the skyscraper still had eighty-six floors, with the top floor an unnumbered one which, as far as most people knew, didn't even exist.

The building management had gone so far as to run excursions to this eighty-sixth floor—it had been the eighty-fifth before elimination of thirteen. The excursionists, of course, had been curious folk who wanted to see what had been the headquarters of the famous man of bronze.

The establishment consisted of three distinct departments: a reception room containing a remarkable inlaid table and a great safe, a library with thousands of scientific tomes, and a laboratory which was one of the most completely equipped in existence.

"Let's put Vesterate in the library," Monk suggested. The homely chemist glanced at Long Tom, who was escorting Lin Pretti rather callously. The young woman was still handcuffed. "Why be so tough on the girl?" Monk added.

Monk was distinctly an admirer of femininity.

"Yes," put in dapper Ham. "I'll take care of the young lady."

Monk scowled at this. Monk and Ham were, as far as conduct went, perpetually unfriendly. They drew to one side now and engaged in a subdued argument about who was to look after exquisite Lin Pretti. The dispute did not remain subdued for long. They began yelling, then retired to the laboratory and shut the door, declaring they were going to tear each other apart. Chemistry added to the excitement by getting an umbrella someone had left and pursuing the pig, Habeas Corpus.

Big-fisted Renny broke into this uproar.

"Vesterate is talking!" Renny yelled.

Tony Vesterate had regained a species of consciousness. Renny, observing this happening, had hastily gotten all but Lin Pretti out of sight, and was coaching the girl on what questions to ask. Vesterate, being a foreign secret agent, would hardly have talked before strangers. Anyway, Lin Pretti herself was curious as to what had happened to Vesterate.

Renny had a pad of typewriter paper. He was writing his questions on this and holding them where Lin Pretti could see; but Vesterate—not about to move—could not.

Renny wrote on his paper: *How can we catch the Man on the Moon?*

He showed it to the girl, and had a feeling this whole thing was ridiculously melodramatic, while Lin Pretti was reading it, then putting it to Vesterate.

Monk, crouched behind a bookcase close to the leather sofa on which they had placed Vesterate's stretcher, had difficulty understanding the man.

"Only thing—I know—is where they depart from—to go to the moon," was what Monk managed to get.

Renny wrote: *Did they really take you to the moon?*

Eventually Vesterate said, "Yes—took me to the moon—in crater—months—brought me back—" He was having a great deal of difficulty.

Renny wrote: *Why did they bring you back from moon?*

It had struck Renny as odd—he was surprised that anything could seem odd in the face of such incredibilities as prisoners on the moon—that a prisoner should be taken to the moon, then brought back.

"They wanted me—carry story of moon crater—to ruler —scare him," said Vesterate.

Renny, hearing that, felt as if he had at last found something logical. But why had this man escaped from Lurgent's crowd, and why had they headed him off, making such desperate efforts to kill him? That didn't look as if they were sending him to the higher power.

Renny wrote out an inquiry about that.

"I saw something—by which I might identify—the Man on the Moon." There was more of this. Vesterate had observed that the Man on the Moon—who was always masked—wore a medallion depicting Satan sitting on a quarter-moon. He had, in a rage, yelled that this would be a clue by which the Man on the Moon could be found. Vesterate had then concealed a sketch of the medallion in a wound which he had received at the time he was captured.

Vesterate had gone further, though. He had learned then that they were going to kill him. He had escaped by plane and flown for the Spanish Plantation, where he knew his country always kept a secret agent.

"Huh!" Pat gulped. "So it was a plane, and not a meteor!"

They learned then that Vesterate had been shot down that night by pursuing planes of the Man on the Moon and, falling in flames from a great height, escaped only by parachute. The planes, he explained, had followed him from the "rocket depot."

Renny wrote: *Where is this spot?*

The spot was on the desolate Maine coast, an exact number of miles from the Canadian border. It was, apparently, not on the sea itself, but a few miles inshore, in an uninhabited region.

Unfortunately Vesterate faded in the midst of his description of the spot. His unconsciousness was complete, and probably only the hasty administering of stimulants kept him alive.

Lin Pretti seemed to think they should not have let Vesterate weaken himself by talking—she said as much in no uncertain words.

"He may not survive the strain!" she said indignantly.

Pat looked at her coldly. "Young lady, we are trying to find Johnny—William Harper Littlejohn, who uses the biggest words and has the biggest heart of any man in the world. If you'll just pardon my frankness, I'd like to say right here that the lives of every spy your ruler has working wouldn't be worth half of Johnny!"

Pat said this so grimly that Lin Pretti paled and afterward was silent.

An attempt was now made to get in touch with Doc Savage to advise him that Vesterate had revealed the location of the spot from which the Man on the Moon started his space ships.

It proved impossible to contact Doc. There was nothing to do but wait—or take some action on their own initiative. Doc Savage's aides took only a few minutes to decide to send two of their number to Maine. They drew lots.

Monk and Ham got the short straws which meant Maine.

They began assembling equipment and changing into stout woods attire. Monk's gear consisted of ancient corduroy pants, very old shoes and a shirt which had distinctly seen better days. Ham went to the other extreme—a natty outfit from the most exclusive gentlemen's shop in the city. Monk eyed the fine feathers and sniffed.

"That's sure expensive garb you're wearing," Monk said.

"I'm surprised you realize it!" Ham snapped.

"Oh, I know expensive garbage when I see it," Monk grimaced.

"Garbage—" Ham purpled indignantly, and after that the pair fell to insulting each other with violent enthusiasm, and were still at it when they arrived at the river-front warehouse, got in a plane, and headed north toward Maine.

Chapter XIII

THE BACKFIRE

Monk and Ham took their two pets, Habeas Corpus and Chemistry. The chimpanzee and the pig accompanied their owners wherever they went.

The plane was fast—it was one of the combination land-and-sea planes—and they flew high on a compass course which brought them across Connecticut, Massachusetts and on into Maine at more than two hundred miles an hour.

Monk and Ham entertained each other with their perpetual quarrel.

"You bandy-legged baboon!" Ham got around to calling Monk when they entered Maine. "You awful freak of nature!"

"Want me to give you some advice about what'll happen to you if you don't lay off me?" Monk asked darkly.

"I'm all ears."

"So's a jackass," Monk reminded.

The fact that no audience was around to witness their violence seemed to make no difference. At times it seemed they were on the point of landing the plane and slaughtering each other; in fact they agreed mutually to do this a number of times.

Eventually they put their plane down about five miles from their destination. It was now almost dusk. By hurrying, Monk and Ham believed they might check on Tony Vesterate's information before it was too dark to see anything.

The underbrush was thick, and the going became steep,

rocky. There were, Monk grumbled, more thorny bushes here in Maine than in an African jungle. The sun was no longer above the hills, but its light remained, although paling.

They kept a sharp lookout, but discerned no one.

Tramping through the tangled Maine woods, they felt tired; it had been a long day, and they had covered much territory, done many things, thanks to the speed of modern planes. Moreover, they had slept but little the night before, and none at all the previous night, when they had been cooperating with Doc—then acting as Behemoth—in an effort to get to the Man on the Moon by keeping track of Lurgent.

Finally they decided their goal could be only a short distance ahead. They increased caution. A faint grayish spot appeared ahead, and Monk, pointing through the trees, called attention to it. They crept closer. It was a signboard:

DANGER!
POISON GAS EXPERIMENTAL ZONE!

They read this legend, scratched their heads thoughtfully, and exchanged glances. Other signs warned:

KEEP AWAY!

Monk, whispering, said, "It's a gag. Meant to scare people away from the place."

"I hate to agree with you, stupid," Ham said, "but that is my guess too."

They went on past the signboards, and came to a high, woven-wire fence. They debated, wondering if this could be part of a capacity-system burglar alarm. A beaten path, obviously made by deer and other prowling woodland creatures, ran along the edge of the fence.

"Probably they ain't got a capacity alarm there," Monk muttered. "The deer and moose coming close to the fence would run 'em ragged."

So they climbed the fence cautiously, each lifting his pet over. It was much darker.

They went fifty yards farther on and began to observe, in a sharp-sided little valley beyond, a rather large building and something else—something shaped vaguely like a giant flat-topped table, slightly tilted, apparently made of concrete, supported by steel braces at one end, sloping down into the earth at the other end . . .

Suddenly they forgot that, for a man came slamming noisily through the growth—a long, incredibly thin man.

"Johnny!" Monk barked.

William Harper Littlejohn was in a hurry. He was also in no condition for running, being hollow-eyed, battered, bruised, and his skin marred by ugly burns as well. Seeing Monk and Ham, he weaved toward them.

"Got—away!" he gulped. "They're—chasing me!"

When Johnny used words as small as these, his predicament was usually desperate. Monk and Ham saw he was almost out on his feet. They picked him up, tried to carry him together; but Monk, growling impatiently, shouldered the bony archaeologist and geologist alone. They headed, naturally, back toward their plane.

They reached the fence, climbed it.

There was yelling behind them, and the sounds men make when running.

"There they come!" Johnny said.

Monk ran on with Johnny, and Ham, galloping behind, began asking questions.

"What have they been doing to you?" Ham demanded.

"Working on me," Johnny explained. "Trying to find out stuff they could use to get Doc."

"They get much?"

"No," Johnny groaned. "But they would have, eventually. They're better than Yaqui Indians, when it comes to knowing torture methods."

"Why'd they bring you here?" Monk growled.

"I'll be superamalgamated!" Johnny grunted. "Believe it or not, they were going to send me to the moon!"

"*What?*"

"So they said. That is, if I talked, they were going to send me to the moon. Otherwise, they assured me I'd die right here on earth."

Ham fell over a bush, tore a rip in his natty outfit, and groaned more loudly than if his own flesh had been rent.

It was quite dark now. The aides ran into bushes, tangled with low limbs, stumbled often, and could not help but make some noise.

But the sounds of pursuit, while not dying, were not coming any closer either, encouraging the idea that they were going to be able to reach the plane. Once they did that, it would be simple to take off. Monk and Ham were both elated, for they had, they considered, accomplished something of a coup.

True, they had been lucky to meet Johnny—so lucky in fact that Monk was inclined to feel a vague uneasiness.

"Who is this Man on the Moon?" Monk demanded.

"My incomprehension approximates an uncontrovertible neiscience," Johnny said.

Using words like those to state he did not know who the Man on the Moon was, indicated Johnny was improving rapidly.

They reached the plane.

Flashlights blazed on them from all around. Then men walked into the luminance with businesslike automatic rifles.

They gave some advice in low, ugly voices.

Monk and Ham stood very still, taking the advice. Johnny squirmed on Monk's shoulder, then quieted when Monk gritted, "You want us shot?"

They were searched, relieved of all weapons.

Then Lurgent, as vicious-looking as a hawk, appeared, flanked by bodyguards. He came over and glowered at Monk.

"Where is Doc Savage?" he demanded.

"To you," Monk said, "boo!"

Lurgent cursed, slapped Monk hard. Monk howled a terrific howl—he always made enormous noises when fighting—and his feet lashed out. Monk was as agile with his legs as the ape he resembled. Lurgent, hit amidships, flew a few feet, then fell.

A man walked behind Monk and dropped him with a whack from a rifle barrel.

Ham made puzzled faces in the flashlight glare. Obviously, he didn't understand what had happened to them. They had left the plane, found Johnny, returned—it looked simple enough. But here was a trap!

Ham mumbled, "How—how . . ."

Johnny suddenly exploded, "Now I know how I came to escape! They let me get away! That was so you would find me and come back here and be in such a hurry you'd fall into a trap!"

"How did they know we were here?" Ham asked. "Was that fence a capacity alarm?"

Johnny nodded.

Lurgent recovered partially from Monk's kick and heaved up. He seemed angrier when he found Monk was unconscious, but came over and kicked the homely chemist anyway.

"Where's Savage?" he asked Ham.

Ham shook his head. "It just happens that I don't know; but if I did, I sincerely hope I could keep it to myself."

After that, Ham got some rough treatment—ordinary brutality administered with feet, fists and gun barrels.

Ham talked a lot. Ham was a lawyer, and talking was his business; and he was good at it. He went into detail now about a number of things, most of them having to do with penitentiaries, electric chairs, the efficiency of the police, the G-men and Doc Savage. He did not say anything about where Doc Savage might be, which was all they wanted to know.

Lurgent, grim-faced, gave it up and issued some orders.

"Take 'em all back to the rocket depot and hold them," he directed.

Then he went to the plane and examined it, paying particular attention to the amount of fuel in the tank. He nodded solemnly.

"We'll take this ship," he decided aloud and, with six of his men, got into the craft. This was near a capacity load for the plane.

Monk, Ham and Johnny were taken in the direction of the place which had been surrounded with the poison-gas warnings. Chemistry and Habeas, after being tied up, were brought along too.

Lurgent took off in the Doc Savage plane. He flew toward New York, but stopped in Boston for refueling.

It was past midnight when Lurgent slanted the plane down out of the night sky. By this time he had accustomed himself to the controls of the fast craft, and was confident.

He immediately came below the legal limit. Planes are not supposed to fly below a certain height over New York City. But Lurgent was following a deliberate plan.

He headed for the towering skyscraper which housed Doc

Savage's headquarters. Or had housed the headquarters, for Lurgent was not quite sure Doc still had his establishment there. But he was acting on the hunch that the bronze man's aerie still occupied the top floor of the great building, which was easily distinguishable in Manhattan's night.

Three times, Lurgent circled close to the skyscraper. He gunned the motor, retarding the spark, causing great bursts of sound.

He was rewarded by seeing big-fisted Renny, Long Tom and tall Aldace K. O'Hannigan appear at one of the windows.

Arms waved inside the skyscraper window.

Lurgent arched over toward the Hudson River to land the plane.

"They've seen this plane and probably recognized it," Lurgent said grimly to his men. "They won't be suspicious, and we'll finish this up in a hurry."

Chapter XIV

THE STOWAWAY

Inside the laboratory big-fisted Renny rumbled happily. "That's the plane Monk and Ham left in!"

Pale, unhealthy-looking Long Tom nodded. "The fact that Monk is in a happy frame of mind proves they must have found something. They must have gotten Johnny."

Aldace K. O'Hannigan drew in a great sigh, then rubbed at his freckled jaw.

"Och! And may the divil use me onery soul to scare babies with if yonder lads ain't got this cleared up. Faith, I've had me fill of goings-on."

Patricia Savage said shortly, "If you could think of why that medallion is important, it might help."

"Bedad, and ain't I told ye, crossing me dirty heart in the doing of it, that it's all beyond me knowing?"

Lin Pretti snapped, "I don't believe you! I think you are one of the Man on the Moon's organization!"

"Faith, and if you was a man, I'd tear off an arm and box your ears with it, no less."

Lin Pretti glared at O'Hannigan. She had, in the last hours, taken the emphatic attitude that she considered him one of the enemy.

Both Renny and Long Tom were surprised at the violence of her vocal aspersions.

O'Hannigan now grinned amiably at her. There was no sarcasm in his grin. Rather, he seemed to be enjoying himself.

"You're a rascal!" Lin Pretti said wildly.

"Faith, mum, and have I ever denied that me soul is black?" O'Hannigan wanted to know.

Lin Pretti began to tremble and put her head back, as if to scream.

Pretty, competent Pat Savage went over to her, and said grimly, "There are two ways of curing hysteria, darling. One is the method doctors use; and the other is mine." With which, Pat slapped Lin Pretti once, very hard.

Lin Pretti's head rocked with the blow. She recoiled, became pale; but she ceased trembling and lost her momentary tendency to hysteria, brought on by the strain of waiting.

Doc's aides had received no word from the bronze man. In fact, since they had left Doc Savage near Norfolk, Virginia, there had been no communication whatever from him. This was no source of relief. They were fighting a mighty organization, the bronze man's aides knew. One which killed coldly, and which they knew little about.

Their not hearing from the bronze man might mean that he had fallen into a trap, or had become prey to Lurgent's men or any one of other lieutenants of the Man on the Moon's organization. With Doc's death, the bronze man's aides could not help but feel helpless. It would mean they would have to battle a mighty organization alone, an organization that was world-wide and outnumbered them hopelessly.

Lin Pretti opened her mouth to say something, but didn't.

There came a knock on the headquarters door.

Renny swung into the reception room, approached the door, then paused. His long, puritanical face registered a flicker of doubt.

"Holy cow! This may not be—" He raised his great voice. "Who's there?"

The door was a bulletproof steel affair, and there was an elaborate arrangement by which one could observe who was outside in the corridor without unlocking the door. This was accomplished by mirrors, periscope-fashion.

"Me—Monk," said a small voice through the door.

It sounded like Monk. Renny whipped to the viewer through which he could see the corridor.

Lurgent and six other men stood in the passage, holding their hands high above their heads. Their wrists seemed to be tied with ropes. Monk was not in sight, but he was a short fellow and might well be standing behind the others.

Aldace K. O'Hannigan came and stared over Renny's wide shoulder into the corridor viewer.

"Bedad and begorra!" he breathed. "Faith, man, that's divil what tried to buy me out of me little medal that poor Bob Thomas gifted to me. 'Tis the very polecat and none other."

It was plain that he meant Lurgent.

Pat trotted in to see what the excitement might be. She took one glance into the reflector.

"Sillies!" she exclaimed. "Let them in! Monk and Ham have caught the whole gang!"

She leaped for the door.

Renny boomed, "Wait—" But it was too late to finish, Pat having already opened the door. Pat said, "Walk right in, said the spider to the fly!" She was elated, envisioning the end of the mystery.

Lurgent and his six men marched in, but Monk did not appear, and Renny rumbled, "Say, what—" and Lurgent and the others threw the ropes off their wrists, brought their hands down, caught guns which dropped out of their sleeves, pointed the guns at Pat, Renny and the others.

"Oh!" Pat gasped. "Oh! I didn't know—I—*it was my fault!*"

Given another moment of delay, Renny would have investigated the fake prisoners; he had been about to suggest it when Pat had opened the door. Time and time again crooks had tried this trick and many others, so Renny, having a suspicious nature, had been determined to make sure.

Pat was acutely conscious that in opening the door she had allowed herself and the others to fall into the hands of the very ones they were fighting, a bad episode no matter which way she looked at it. Mentally she kicked herself for being such an impetuous fool.

Renny rumbled sourly, "Now you begin to understand why Doc prefers no women messing around in our business."

Pat swallowed, looking disgusted and remorseful.

Lurgent's men disarmed them, then walked through the big headquarters, only to come back and profanely report no trace of Doc Savage.

Lurgent growled, "Take the prisoners down to the plane. It's late enough at night that nobody will notice anything wrong."

"The plane we came in won't hold us all," a man reminded.

"I had the Man on the Moon send another ship," Lurgent snapped. "It'll be down on the river by the time we are."

The prisoners were bound.

"What about Vesterate?" a man asked.

Lurgent went over and looked down at Tony Vesterate, frowned, then held the green man's wrist for a while. He dropped the wrist and wiped his fingers on his trousers leg, as if cleaning them of something invisible.

"Dead," he said. "And hell, we won't take the body."

Renny, Long Tom and Pat exchanged glances, but did not say anything. Vesterate was not dead. He was in a coma which was very close to death, and resembled it as well.

Lurgent's men, by boldness, got their captives to the waterfront without incident, or almost without incident, for none of them noticed one small thing which happened. A shadowy shape that appeared twice—the first time as they were leaving the eighty-six-story skyscraper by a side door, and appearing again in swift motion behind the two taxicabs, the drivers of which had been slugged and lay bound and gagged on the floorboards.

A second plane was waiting on the Hudson. The two craft were soon loaded and in the air, heading northeast toward the Maine coast.

It was still dark when the ships slanted down toward what Lurgent had called the "rocket depot." Two great floodlights furnished good illumination. Renny, craning his neck as the craft banked, observed what had seemed to be a giant, flat-topped table, placed at a tilt. It was a concrete apron, a huge thing. At the lower end of this slanting stretch of cement was a round hole, not quite a score of feet in diameter, which resembled nothing so much as the magnified maw of a single-barreled shotgun. This seemed to be embedded in a great mass of concrete and steel.

The planes landed on the floodlighted apron. Doc's amphibian, being smaller and faster than the other craft, had a high landing speed. As a result, it overrolled the apron and piled up in some brush with one wing askew. The passengers, however, were only slightly shaken.

The mishap had occurred outside the floodlighted area.

Lurgent and his men produced flashlights, and by that illumination unloaded the captives.

"Take 'em into the depot," Lurgent ordered.

"What about this wrecked plane?"

"Dissemble it and get rid of it tomorrow."

Doc Savage's men, Pat, Lin Pretti and O'Hannigan were herded close together by the menace of rifles.

Lin Pretti glared at O'Hannigan. "Why are you keeping up this pretense?"

"Och! And what might ye be meaning, mum?"

"You're one of the Man on the Moon's gang! Why have them pretend you're not?"

Lurgent walked up and shoved Lin Pretti. "Fasten that tongue if you don't want it cut off!"

The prisoners were moved toward the great concrete mass in which the huge barrel was embedded.

Quiet now descended on the valley. Lurgent and the others walked around to the north side of the concrete mass, where there was an open door. They entered. The floodlights went out. Although it was a moonlight night, the darkness which followed the dousing of the lights seemed doubly intense.

During that interval of intense black, there was a faint stirring in the buoyancy compartment, boat-shaped, which comprised the amphibian's streamlined float. This compartment was closed with a watertight hatch, the hatch being of some size because it was customary to store supplies there. The hatch opened.

Doc Savage got out of the float interior, and glided silently toward the concrete mass.

Chapter XV

MOON-BOUND

Doc Savage had lived, considering the incredible dangers of his strange profession, a long time—although he was a young man. He took no chances, which accounted in part for his continued presence on earth. He frequently did not tell even his five aides or Pat what he intended doing, or where he would be. He did not distrust them. But there was always a chance they would be tricked into revealing his whereabouts to an enemy, or a foe might capture one of them and force admissions.

The truth was that Doc had been keeping a close watch on his four aides. Not checking on them, however. He had been watching Aldace K. O'Hannigan to ascertain if the man made a move which would admit guilt.

A witness to the raid on his headquarters by Lurgent, Doc had not interfered—once convinced his aides were not to be killed—but had followed the raiders and their prisoners to the planes. In the darkness it had been simple to swim out, open the float hatch and crawl inside.

It was possible Lurgent might lead the way to the Man on the Moon.

All of which accounted for Doc's presence, in a few moments after the floodlights went out, beside the titanic mass of concrete. He listened at the door, which had been left open.

There was a passage beyond the door, Doc entered, and heard voices.

Lurgent was saying, "Come on, come on! Get into those suits!"

The voice came out of an open door, from a room in which there was light. Doc Savage, silent as a bronze cloud, drifted past the door, and his eyes, in the brief moment that they roamed over the interior, saw that Lurgent was forcing the prisoners, one at a time, to don a strange skintight green garment.

This green suit seemed to be made of layers of silk, and it was equipped with a metal ring at the neck, on which a helmet evidently was to be secured with wing nuts.

The helmets lay on the floor, bulbous things of shiny metal, fitted with attachments of rubber and metal. Metal belts lay on the floor, and these were equipped with devices to supply oxygen to the helmets.

To get into the green suits, it was necessary for Monk and Renny, the biggest of Doc's aides, to get rid of most of their clothing.

Pat and Lin Pretti hastily turned their backs.

It appeared the suit-donning would take some time, so Doc continued on down the passage. He had used a knife and opened a rip in the plane float, but what he had seen through that had only interested him the more intensely.

The passage was closed by a door, a shiny thing—all the metal used here seemed to be the new stainless kind—and the bronze man grasped the handle of the portal. His pull opened the door, which proved to be of unusual shape inside, curved to fit the round barrel embedded in the great concrete block.

Immediately beyond lay another door. Doc examined it. There seemed to be something like a huge bullet fitted inside the barrel, a giant thing of shiny alloy metal. The second door admitted to this when Doc tested it.

He stepped into what might have been the main cabin of the rocket—if this was what the thing was. It was equipped with seats, but these were strange things. They consisted literally of deeply upholstered molds for human bodies; and these were suspended on all sides by great springs, which were fastened to metal struts and girders.

Apparently the seats were designed to cushion the force of terrific shocks.

This much was discernible only vaguely by the light which

came from the passage. Doc entered the thing, after hesitating, and began feeling his way about, exploring

He had not gotten far when there was some sound in the passage. Hurriedly the bronze man scrambled aft. Someone was approaching.

Doc Savage entertained no doubts about being discovered if he could not find concealment. They were sure to see him. His sensitive fingers raced. He trained those fingers, as he trained each part of his remarkable body in daily exercise. In the case of his fingertips, the exercise usually consisted of rapid reading of Braille—the printing system for the blind, which consists of upraised dots.

The bronze man found what seemed to be a locker. He opened it too quickly, causing a squeak. After that he listened, but the sound must have been covered by the scuff of approaching feet, and the squeaky, childlike voice of Monk, who was saying, "Before this is over, I'm gonna knock some heads loose!"

Doc explored with his hands, found the locker empty, and got inside. It was, he discovered, ventilated with slits, so it must be a clothes locker. He closed the door.

Monk was shoved roughly into the interior of the strange device inside the big barrel.

"Quit shovin' me!" he roared.

He looked unusually ridiculous in his green tights.

Shortly afterward, Ham was also propelled into the chamber. Ham also wore green tights, but managed to carry them rather dapperly. He frowned critically at Monk.

"*Ur-r-r-roak*! *Ur-r-r-roak*!" he said.

Monk stared blankly. "Hey, what the heck?"

"Oh! You speak English?"

"Huh?"

"You look so much like a frog in that gear I thought you might speak the language," Ham explained.

"You shyster!" Monk gritted. "This ain't no time to make cracks!"

The truth probably was that Ham had been taking his mind off his predicament by insulting Monk.

Shortly afterward, Long Tom, Renny, Johnny and Pat were propelled into the chamber. They were followed by Lin Pretti and big red Aldace K. O'Hannigan. The latter was rumbling angrily.

"Sure, and this thing is beginnin' to tug at the O'Hannigan dander!" he complained. "Take yer hands off me, ye divil scuts!"

"Kick his ribs in if he don't shut up!" Lurgent ordered.

Lin Pretti stared at O'Hannigan as if beginning to doubt that he belonged to the gang of the Man on the Moon.

None of the prisoners as yet wore any helmets.

"Listen to me!" Lurgent yelled.

They listened to him.

For a few moments Lurgent did not say anything; then he chuckled harshly.

"I'll make this short. We've decided not to kill you. As a matter of fact, we don't get rid of valuable prisoners—people we may be able to use in the future."

O'Hannigan roared, "Faith, and ye'll regret . . ."

"Shut up!" Lurgent rasped. "We're sending you where we send all our prisoners: to the moon!"

Renny, the engineer, who was also something of an amateur astronomer, rumbled, "This stuff about going to the moon is crazy as crystal gazing!"

Lurgent shrugged. "What you think doesn't concern us at all. We think we put you on the moon. And either we do, or we've been fooling ourselves a long time."

He paused and gave an order. His men fell upon the prisoners and strapped them in the cushioned chairs. Monk, who liked to fight, proceeded to do so, but did not accomplish much except to his own damage.

When all the prisoners were fastened, Lurgent made another loud speech.

"This is a spaceship!" he hollered. "It is launched by explosives, just as a bullet is driven from a gun. Then, for the first few hundred miles out into space, burning gases from stern vents propel it in rocket fashion. This gas propulsion is decreased, for momentum is a tremendously powerful force out in space where there is less gravity pull."

He paused long enough for this to soak in.

"The ship is equipped with folding wings, just as is a plane. These wings are opened out mechanically as the rocket feels the gravitation of the moon."

He scowled at the prisoners. "Now, in order that none of you shall learn exactly how this operates, in case you would think of capturing one like it on the moon and escaping, it is necessary to make you unconscious for the duration of the trip."

He waved at his men. Instantly, they scrambled out of the strange cabin.

Lurgent stood alone inside. From a pocket he brought a glass bottle which contained liquid and was corked. He pulled the cork.

Doc Savage came out of the locker. He distrusted the stuff in the bottle.

Lurgent saw Doc. He smashed the bottle on the metal, sprang backward, and got the iron door shut. Doc hit it. He was too late; Lurgent had it fastened on the other side.

Doc Savage, holding his breath, worked at the door, but gave it up as hopeless. He lunged forward. There was a door, apparently leading into another compartment, but it was locked, and too stout for his unaided hands. He tried aft. The same thing there.

His eyes stung. His lungs ached. More than three minutes had passed now, and although he could hold his breath an unusually long time, the violent exertion he had been putting forth had used up the oxygen in his lungs.

When Doc finally had to breathe in, it was as if fumes stronger than ammonia had gone into his lungs; then a roaring came into his ears, and a tiny crackling, after which his heart seemed to pump blackness into his eyes and keep pumping until all his being was filled with dizzy sepia.

He barely felt the hardness of the floor when he fell against it.

Chapter XVI

MOON PIT

Doc Savage awakened slowly, as from a sleep, but there was a strong subconscious impression that it had been a long time since he fell gassed.

His watch had stopped. It had run down, and not broken, he saw, and realized this meant he had been out at least twenty-four hours. How much longer was problematical.

Doc felt very hungry. At least a three-day hunger feeling, he estimated. But even that was deceptive, because unconscious persons can be fed while they are senseless.

It was not possible to tell from the sun how long he had been out. As a matter of fact, there seemed to be no sun. The bronze man stood up hastily to see about that.

He instantly became so dizzy that he had to crouch on hands and knees, and let his head clear, as well as get coordination into his muscles.

He now wore one of the green suits, he perceived. It fitted his great frame rather tightly. He did not, though, wear a helmet and no helmet was in sight. His head cleared, and he arose again.

He was lying inside a perfectly square stone room which had a low door at one side. The stone room was equipped with a shelf, on which lay several neatly folded blankets. Doc had been lying on the floor.

Doc passed out of the naked stone chamber by stooping and wedging himself through the door.

Outside, he found neither daylight nor night. Rather, it was a strange half light, grayish and unreal, shot through at times with a faintly orange glow. With great interest he surveyed the surroundings.

He stood on a perfectly flat floor of rock perhaps two hundred yards across. On this stood almost a score of square stone blocks which were probably huts.

Stone walls rose vertically on all sides, lifted as sheer as the sides of a cup for hundreds of feet. The walls looked rugged, unclimbable.

On the left—about eighty feet above the floor of the cup —there was a shelf. On this stood a long stone building. A man in green tights paced in front of the structure, along the edge of the shelf. He carried a rifle and glanced downward frequently, indicating he was a sentry.

Doc Savage gave attention to the sky again.

It did not look like any sky on earth.

The big bronze man walked over to the wall below the shelf. There seemed to be no way of climbing. The guard above glanced down idly, but kept his rifle ready.

"Where is this place?" Doc asked sharply.

The sentry only laughed shortly.

Again, the bronze man's eyes roved curiously. The stone all about was dark, apparently volcanic, and looked hard enough to have a little glass melted into it.

Doc Savage turned and walked away from the wall. Apparently he was not to be harmed physically. They had brought him here, of course, after finding him senseless in the rocket, as Lurgent had called it. To tell the truth, he was more than slightly surprised that he was still alive.

Coming to one of the blocklike stone huts, Doc stooped and looked in.

Monk and Ham sprawled listlessly inside. The pig, Habeas, and the chimp, Chemistry, were also in the hut. The presence of the two animals was enough of a surprise to draw briefly from Doc Savage the small, trilling sound which he made in moments of mental stress. Monk and Ham, hearing the sound, glanced up quickly. They had merely been resting, and were not unconscious.

"Whew!" Monk groaned. "How on earth can you move around, Doc? Me and Ham are sicker'n dogs."

"How long have you been conscious?" Doc Savage asked.

"About twenty-four hours," Monk mumbled.

Doc said, "I just came out of it."

Monk explained, "They gave you several extra shots of that gas on account of they were scared of you."

"How long have we been prisoners?"

"More than a week, everybody seems to figure."

Doc Savage's eerie trilling rose and fell briefly, then died; and the bronze man said, "How many of us are here?"

"The whole crowd."

"Harmed?"

"Not much. They feel kind of lousy. But the other prisoners tell us that wears off in a few days."

Doc said, "Other prisoners?"

"Sure," Monk said painfully. "There's at least twenty other people here."

"Where," the bronze man asked quietly, "are we supposed to be?"

"On the moon."

Doc Savage stepped out of the square stone hut quickly, for he wanted to see these other prisoners and ask them why they were there. This strange crater had an eerie fascination, an ominous air.

The air was quite cold, the bronze man noted. Almost bitingly chill. There was, in addition, a strange odor in the atmosphere. It was hardly noticeable, and in fact had escaped his attention for a time, probably because his olfactory organs were accustomed to it when he regained consciousness.

He suddenly realized another thing: he must have a fever, which had made the air seem even warmer than it actually was. The thing that convinced him of this was a pail of water standing beside the hut door; but instead of water in the pail, there was a solid lump of ice.

Also, there seemed to be a little snow sifting over the rim of the crater—for crater this place seemed to be.

Patricia Savage appeared and met Doc. She put her hand to her head and grimaced.

"I never thought I'd see the moon under these conditions," she said gloomily.

Doc looked at her silently.

"Go ahead," Pat urged. "Tell me that if I hadn't been so insistent on some excitement, I wouldn't be here."

Pat, the bronze man observed, was under a strain, so he gave her a smile which was gentle, genuine and encouraging.

"Tony Vesterate apparently got away from the place," he reminded her.

Pat said, a little more carefully, "Thanks, Doc." She waved an arm at the other huts. "I'll introduce you around."

The first of the other prisoners was a quiet, highly educated gentleman of past middle age—a Japanese. Until a little less than two years ago, he had been a world figure in diplomacy. He was supposed to know a great deal about the policies of his nation. He had disappeared unexpectedly, after which there had been rumors of assassination.

The next prisoner was a prominent judge from the City of New York, who had vanished unexpectedly, and for no reason that anyone had ever been able to discover. There had been many false rumors of this judge being discovered, but he had never been found, of course. The judge happened to be an expert on American law.

The third prisoner was a high-ranking general in the French army. He knew more than any other man, probably, about the French military organization.

These captives were a fair sample of all the prisoners. The total nearly reached a score.

Each prisoner had learned too much about the organization of the Man on the Moon. Usually, they had learned this in the course of their duties for their respective governments.

It now became clear that the Man on the Moon ordinarily assassinated those who menaced him. But in cases where the dangerous person had knowledge which could prove of value, the unfortunate was seized and brought here.

Each captive insisted that this spot was a crater on the moon.

There was a listlessness, a hopeless give-up-to-it-all air about most of the captives. They were on the moon, well guarded, living under terrible conditions, for it was always bitterly cold.

Most of them, Doc learned, had reached a point of surrender where they gave information freely to their captors—information which was no doubt valuable to the Man on the Moon.

The bronze man began to get an even clearer conception of the Man on the Moon's organization. Espionage—spying —was no small part of his profession.

That interested Doc, because it clarified finally the thing

which had first brought him into this weird affair: the fact that someone had been masquerading as Doc's men and flying over the fortified areas of Europe. The Man on the Moon's organization had simply masqueraded as Doc's crowd to photograph fortified areas for some other power for which they happened to be working at the minute.

As Doc Savage's physical condition became more normal, throwing off the aftereffects of the gas, he was more and more aware of the intense cold. Like the other prisoners, he began to keep inside the stone huts.

Food, he learned, was lowered to the prisoners twice daily from the ledge. The giant bronze man partook of the food with the others, behaving meekly, because he did not yet have a plan of action.

"Have you any idea why they kept us alive?" he asked big-fisted Renny.

"Holy cow, no!" Renny rumbled.

Doc observed Lin Pretti and Aldace K. O'Hannigan in conversation, and walked over to them. It appeared that Lin Pretti had changed her mind about O'Hannigan being one of the enemy.

"I'm sorry I tried to make you think Mr. O'Hannigan was one of them," the girl said.

The freckled Aldace K. O'Hannigan grinned. "Sure, an' I've put me spell on the gurl and made her change her mind. It's a pleasant job I'm findin' it, no less."

Doc was no mind reader, but it seemed that Lin Pretti and O'Hannigan were beginning to like each other.

"Anything you can give in the line of information?" the bronze man asked.

"No, sor, divil a bit." O'Hannigan shook his scarlet head. "Och! It's an ache me head has from trying to figure out what part was played by that little medal with a picture of a divil sittin' on the moon."

"No idea about who the Man on the Moon might be?"

"Not a one, bedad!"

Doc Savage left them, joined some of the other prisoners, and engaged in conversation. He found it a little difficult to probe them out of their listlessness, so as to secure information.

He did learn that the rockets evidently landed somewhere

else; not many miles from the crater, however. None of the captives had secured a chance to examine the rockets closely.

Later, Doc Savage devoted many minutes to watching the strangely gray sky. Snow was really swirling over the edges of the crater now, but the sky was still leaden in tint, with occasional glowing effects.

The Japanese diplomat came over, accompanied by the French general. The latter said, "Eef you 'ave ze interest to know, m'sieu', thees volcano cone are on side of moon which 'as never been seen from earth."

Doc asked, "How do you know that?"

The other shrugged elaborately. "We 'ave been told, *oui*."

Doc said, "The air does not seem just the way scientists have decided the air on the moon should be—if there is any air."

"As 'ave been explain to us," said the general. "Science ees not too exact. Zey make mistakes, *oui*? You 'ave smell something strange in air, *non*?"

Doc admitted he had detected a quality of queerness in the atmosphere.

"Oxygen," explained the general. "Eet ees put into air from ledge all time, or we die soon."

The pipe from which the oxygen came was pointed out to Doc by the Frenchman. It was high up on the cliff, pointed downward, made a steady hissing; and the distinct odor was stronger below it.

In the course of time it became apparent that neither day nor night in the commonly accepted worldly sense existed inside the pit.

Doc was discussing that with Monk and Ham when a shout rang from the ledge.

"Doc Savage!" the voice called. "The Man on the Moon is ready to talk to you!"

Chapter XVII

AIMLESS?

Doc Savage went to a spot below the ledge. A noosed rope was tossed down; he placed this under his arms, and was hauled upward. Guards menaced him with small automatic pistols which had been converted into semimachine guns. It was significant that they had these weapons handcuffed to their wrists, presumably to prevent the weapons being seized unexpectedly and turned on their owners.

The bronze man was conducted into a long room. The roof was supported by a single post, and to this post was attached a chain. The other end of the chain was padlocked around the bronze man's waist.

A door at the other end of the room opened. A man came out—a rather large man, neatly dressed. Across the man's chest was draped a heavy gold watch chain, and to this chain was affixed a gold medallion, rectangular, with rounded corners, and bearing the likeness of Satan seated on one corner of a quarter-moon.

The stranger's head was completely concealed in a metal helmet, evidently one of the helmets made to be attached to the green suits. Only the eyes were discernible through the helmet window, which had been blocked off—except for a slit—by adhesive tape.

The helmet wearer now did an unexpected thing: one hand —it was gloved—detached the medallion from the watch chain, raised the thing and shoved it under the edge of the helmet. It was plain that the helmet wearer put the medallion between his teeth and held it there on edge to disguise his voice.

"I shall explain why you were kept alive," he told Doc Savage.

The voice was well disguised by the metal, and also by the hollow acoustics of the helmet's interior.

Doc said quietly, "You are the Man on the Moon, so-called?"

"Naturally," said the other.

"What do you want?"

"You will tell me where your personal records can be found," ordered the Man on the Moon. "I know you have an international organization for gathering information. I know also that you own many valuable chemical formulas, and mechanical secrets of military value. I know you have planes which are faster and more maneuverable than any fighting plane today. I want the designs of those too."

The disguised voice turned into an elated chuckling.

"You are going to be able to do me a great deal of good," the voice said when the mirth subsided.

Doc said, "I hardly think there is need of discussing this."

"You are not ready to cooperate?"

The bronze man did not trouble to answer.

The Man on the Moon leveled an arm. "Put him back. He'll be glad enough to talk later on."

He retreated back through the door, pulling it shut after him.

The men carefully opened the padlock which held the chain around Doc Savage's middle. The bronze man was lowered back into the pit.

A number of the prisoners in the crater were waiting anxiously, which indicated those visits of the captives to the ledge had occurred before, with unpleasant results.

Doc Savage seemed preoccupied. He did not say much until, some time later, he got one of the older prisoners aside.

"Describe your trip here in that rocket," the bronze man requested.

The captive did so. His story corresponded approximately with the bronze man's own experience, with the difference that the fellow had revived during the trip through space, as he explained it. There had been a great roaring inside the rocket, and it was hot, as if heated by friction as it passed through space at terrific speed.

"How about when you landed here?" Doc asked.

"I was made senseless again," the other replied. "Lurgent explained that it was their policy not to allow any of the captives to learn too much about how the rocket was operated."

When Doc Savage consulted some of the other captives, he received almost identical stories. They did not seem to care to discuss it. The idea of being on the moon plainly depressed them to the point of utter hopelessness.

Doc put one more question to each of them.

"When the Man on the Moon talks to you, he always disguises his voice with that gold medal?" the bronze man queried. "He holds it between his teeth."

It seemed this was the usual procedure.

Homely Monk put an inquiry to Doc later. He was curious about the purpose of the bronze man's questions concerning the medal.

"Merely checking up on why Tony Vesterate made the sketch of the medal," Doc explained. "The Man on the Moon apparently has a habit of carrying it on his watch chain. It is a distinctive medal, and he could be identified by it."

"He could quit wearing it, couldn't he?" Monk countered.

"Of course. And he probably has. But if he wore it in the past, someone might remember the fact, and that would be the tipoff."

"*Um-m-m.* Seems a kind of thin reason for him to go to so much trouble trying to catch Vesterate."

"The Man on the Moon is a fellow who does not take chances where his own identity is concerned."

Nothing happened for some hours. Another meal was lowered to the prisoners. It was the custom of the captives to retire to their huts after eating, there being little else to do.

Doc spoke a few words and, as a result, his entire party congregated for a while, then drifted apart, roaming in the gray half light. In fact, they wandered around, distracting attention, and eventually they all ended up by passing close to the side of a certain hut, one at a time.

A flat stone comprised part of the side of this hut. On the stone, using a hard rock, Doc had scratched some instructions.

After all his aides had read the orders, the bronze man drifted by and obliterated them.

Something like ten hours later, the wind died. It grew very quiet.

After the wind fell, Doc Savage moved over to the edge of the pit, not far from the ledge. The snow had drifted a few inches deep here. It was fine stuff, like flour, and smooth.

The bronze man proceeded to walk, shuffling his feet, plowing a groove in the snow. He walked straight some of the time, made circles often, and grooved letters in the snow —letters all four feet high.

No one noticed this.

Doc went back to his hut. He was whistling a light tune.

Long Tom, the electrical wizard, had been waiting for that tune. The instructions on the rock had directed him to do so, and also to make the move which he now made.

Long Tom walked over and stood beside the letters which Doc had drawn in the snow. Naturally, he read them. He emitted a gulp of astonishment, and his eyes almost popped. Then he waited tensely for Doc Savage's next move.

The broze man, in his hut, had stripped off the green suit. Lurgent's men had taken his outer garments. But they had left him his socks, shorts and undershirt, doubtless having searched these silken—or they appeared to be silk—garments thoroughly.

Doc removed the undershirt.

He put the rest of the garments back on.

There were a few matches in each hut—the miserable prison cubicles were equipped with kerosene lamps which gave some warmth when the cold became bitterest. Doc got the matches in his hut.

A careful survey through the door showed that the sentry on the ledge was now alert. He was staring at Long Tom, but due to the bad light, was unable to see what was written in the snow.

Doc went outside.

"There are no matches in my hut!" he called to the sentry. "Get me some!"

The matches were all in the bronze man's pocket.

The sentry stared, said something uncomplimentary. Doc

repeated his demand for matches. It was the custom of the sentry to enter the shed on the ledge and ask what to do about it whenever a prisoner made a demand. He did this now.

Doc Savage raced over and stood, unobserved, under the ledge. It was, unfortunately, a vertical wall above him, but there was no overhang to conceal him in case the sentry came back and looked down.

Long Tom, following the orders scraped on the rock, took care of that.

The instant the sentry reappeared, Long Tom began to yell. He created a great commotion.

"Look here!" he yelled. "Somebody's written the name of the Man on the Moon in the snow!"

That got the sentry's attention. He turned a powerful flashlight on Long Tom.

"Damn my soul!" the sentry exploded, and ran back into the shed, yelling for his chief to come and look.

Doc Savage struck matches and applied them to the undershirt. He struck several matches, got it aflame as quickly as he could. He held it as high as possible, and held his breath.

A violently yellow smoke came from the burning undershirt. Plainly, it was impregnated with chemicals. When he could no longer hold it, Doc tossed it upward, then retreated a few paces.

His flake-gold eyes were now streaming tears.

The voice of the Man on the Moon began yelling curses above. Then came commands for a man to descend quickly and obliterate what was written in the snow.

Long Tom promptly ran from where he had been standing. It was fortunate he did so, because they began shooting at him. He got under cover behind a hut before he was hit.

A rope came snaking down the cliff from the shelf. Then a man appeared, sliding hurriedly down it. He came into the cloud of rising gas—it was a variety of tear gas only—and began to curse. In his agony, he came down much faster than he intended, and hit the floor of the pit rather heavily.

Doc was waiting for him. A single stroke of the bronze fist put the man to sleep.

Doc seized the rope, climbed. He kept his eyes shut. The tear gas would be greatly dissipated by the time it reached the top, and would not blind anyone completely. But the bronze man was depending on the discomfiture it would create.

What shaking he caused on the rope must have been mistaken by those above for the man still descending. They kept their lights on Long Tom's shelter, and were still shooting. That helped Doc reach the top without being discovered.

The bronze man swung over the ledge. Men were coughing, rubbing their eyes. Doc had guessed correctly. They were not blinded, only in pain.

The Man on the Moon did not recognize Doc for a moment.

"What are you coming back for?" he snarled. "Get down there and rub that out before . . ."

Then he barked in fright, started to raise his gun. Doc, diving, hit the nearest man. The fellow was driven back by the shock, and hit his chief. The Man on the Moon was knocked off balance, and instead of trying to remain and fight, wheeled and pitched for the door of his shed.

Three men were on the ledge now. Others, it seemed, were inside the long building on the ledge. They were shouting, wanting to know what had happened.

Doc came around, made for one of the three men on the ledge. The fellow was standing foolishly, not realizing what it was all about, squinting his eyes. Doc struck. The man's jaw gave on one side, crunching, and he began turning around slowly, dizzily.

Doc veered for the other two men. They sprang backward, wildly frightened and confused, and one of them slipped off the edge of the shelf, but grabbed his fellow and hung on, screaming. The two became very occupied with each other, trying to keep from going over the edge.

Down on the pit floor, Doc's men were racing for the rope. They began climbing.

Doc Savage came around and flung for the door of the building on the ledge. It was closed. He grasped the fastening. There was a thump inside, a shot—for a bullet came through the wood—and the Man on the Moon squalled profanely.

To try entering by the door would invite suicide. The bronze man whipped along the side of the building, rounded the corner. There was a window. He knocked the sash in, brushed out the glass with an elbow, the thick green suit protecting him from the sharp edges.

Inside the room—it was evidently a barracks of some kind —men yelled profanely. Light came on as one put a hand on a light switch. In the illumination, Doc discerned many men, and a gun rack, well filled, near the door. The men apparently had been asleep, and were yanking on clothing before they went out in the bitter cold—at least trying to get into coats.

Doc dived into the room. He scooped up a wooden canned-goods box, threw it, and the electric light bulb exploded.

The fight which followed was noisy and black. Doc crossed the room, met three men, who took hold of him with enthusiasm. The four of them went down. Fists struck. Feet kicked. Doc's corded metal fingers twisted and poked and dug. Then he heaved free and got to the gun cabinet.

Another man had already reached the gun rack. Doc fought with him. But the bronze man, possessing senses infinitely superior—thanks to their scientific development—had an advantage. The man at the gun rack retreated, squalling that he had a broken arm, in a moment.

Doc got the guns, an armload of them. He began pitching them out through the window. When his hands were empty, he maneuvered over and yanked open the door of the room in which the Man on the Moon had taken shelter.

Light glared in that room. Doc retreated quickly from the illumination, stumbled over a chair, picked it up and, shooting it accurately through the door, extinguished the other light.

The Man on the Moon fired his gun in wild nervousness.

An attacker, leaping, came down upon Doc. The bronze man fell. Then he turned, got the fellow's throat, and tried to throw him off. He did not succeed.

No one was more surprised than the bronze man. His strength—a reservoir carefully filled by long training—was something he had come to depend upon. But now, at a critical moment, it was failing him.

A second man fell upon him. A third. Then others. They beat him. He struck back, his blows still harder than any they landed, but not hard enough to be effective against such odds. He was weakening. He knew, of course, the long period under the effects of the gas was responsible. The stuff had been worse than he had expected.

There was shouting around the ledge building, the pound of running feet. Then Monk, huge and apelike, piled through the broken window, whooping in anticipation of the fight.

Renny wrenched open the outer door of the chamber in which the Man on the Moon stood. The latter's rifle smacked. Renny roared and stumbled back, grabbing at his chest. He went down, bawling, "Holy cow!" foolishly.

Someone put a knife into Doc's right leg. The agony of that washed all through the bronze giant. He got hold of the knife wrist and fought to keep the blade from finding a more vital spot.

Long Tom and Ham piled into the fight via the window. Then the big Aldace K. O'Hannigan.

"Och!" O'Hannigan howled. "Kill the divils!"

There was roaring and screeching inside the room, the breaking of furniture and the falling of bodies, the smashing of fists, the other sounds men make when trying to kill each other bare-handed.

The melee ended when Lurgent—he had been very silent and inconspicuous during the fight—tried to get out of the room. He succeeded, joined his chief, the Man on the Moon, and they ran out of the house on the ledge.

The huge red O'Hannigan followed them, not through the door, but out through the window. He picked up a rifle.

"No killing!" Doc called, and his voice, compared to its usual volume, was weak.

There were two shots, close together, from O'Hannigan's rifle.

Then O'Hannigan came back and poked his rifle in the window.

"Gimme room!" he directed. "Faith, and I'll get me some more skunks!"

That was the final straw. The survivors of the Man on the Moon gang fled wildly through the door.

Doc Savage, trying to follow them, stumbled and went down, dizzy and weak, nearer complete collapse than at any time in a long part of his strange, perilous career.

Monk and the others chased the fugitives.

Patricia Savage, aided by Lin Pretti, was stemming the flow from Doc's knife wound when Monk and the others came back. The wound would not be fatal, but it would hinder Doc's walking for quite a few days to come.

Monk, more than ever resembling a green frog in his tights, stamped inside.

"They got away," he complained. "Man, they've got half a dozen big long-distance planes and a couple of hangars about a mile from here!"

"The other planes safe?" Doc asked quickly.

"Oh, sure," Monk said gloomily.

"What about Lurgent and the Man on the Moon?"

"They're lying out behind," Monk explained.

"Bedad, you didn't think I missed 'em, did ye?" asked O'Hannigan. "Me, thot was the best shot in me regiment!"

Monk muttered that Lurgent and his chief were dead enough, but that didn't help things any, and that although they did have airplanes, what good would airplanes do when they were on the moon?

Big-fisted Renny emitted a loud snort. "Aren't you wise to that fake yet?"

"Yes, you missing link," Ham promptly told Monk, "aren't you wise?"

Monk scowled at Ham. "You aren't wise, either. A minute ago, you were groaning about living on the moon the rest of your life." Monk looked at Renny. "You mean we're not on the moon?"

Renny glanced at Doc. "Want to explain that, Doc?"

"We're not on the moon," the bronze man said. "Too many things were different from what science has decided the moon would be like. Gravity, for one. And the air. You realize now that you are not breathing oxygen pumped into the pit."

"Huh!" Monk blinked. "Well—blazes! That's right! And I still feel all right."

"Renny," Doc suggested, "you might take a look at that pipe."

Renny departed, searching, examining, and after a time came back with the explanation, "They were just pumping some smelly stuff through the pipe. It's carbon monoxide to depress the people in the pit, and some chemical to make it smell. Just a gag!"

"Then the whole moon business was just a gag!" Monk roared indignantly. "And I thought . . ."

Doc said, "An elaborate trick, cleverly executed, to make the prisoners think they were being taken to the moon. The idea undoubtedly was to depress the captives, make them give information more readily. You yourselves saw how it worked."

Monk sighed. "It sure did. Man, I sure felt low at the idea of being on the moon!" He glanced outside at the cold and the snow. "I didn't like the climate. *Say*, where are we, anyhow?"

They did not find that out until they questioned one of the prisoners. This fellow revealed that the crater was situated on the deserted western shore of Greenland.

The twilight effect was due to the fact that the sun, in the Polar regions, did not get directly overhead, but remained below the horizon for half the year, and just above it the other half. The six-months-night-and-six-months-day effect, as Monk commented, grinning at his earlier fears.

Lin Pretti, as they questioned the prisoner, went to the edge of the ledge to put a flashlight beam on the name which Doc had tracked into the snow below—the name of the Man on the Moon.

She came back looking shocked, unbelieving.

"I just saw—" She passed a hand over her eyes. "But he—that man—was killed at that inlet near the Spanish Plantation."

"Not really killed," Doc corrected. "The Man on the Moon was caught by his own men, none of whom really knew his identity. He told Lurgent who he was, and Lurgent pretended to kill him, and throw his body in the lake."

"Doc!" Monk exploded. "When did you first discover this? I mean, when did you suspect it?"

"When the sketch of the medal turned up," Doc replied, "and we found that O'Hannigan was wearing one, which had been given him."

The bronze man and his aides proceeded with final arrangements for getting back to the States. The prisoners were then brought out of the crater, those who could not climb themselves. It would be necessary to make more than one trip by plane, of course, but that would not be difficult.

Monk had to climb down and pick up Habeas, as the pig couldn't climb. As for Chemistry, Ham merely called and the ape came up the rope like a veteran, looking oddly like Monk. Both aides had left their pets in the crater because of the danger of gunfire.

Doc Savage worked on the prisoners, questioning them. They were willing to talk after a little persuasion. Doc learned much of the Man on the Moon's organization from them, and from the records that were unearthed on the ledge. Enough, altogether, to effectively smash the great organization and recapture the escaped men.

Aldace K. O'Hannigan did two things before they departed. The first disgusted Monk and Ham no little. The Irishman announced that he and Lin Pretti were engaged, and that the young lady was surely not going to do any more secret agent work.

Secondly, O'Hannigan buried the Man on the Moon. He did much muttering about what inscription to put on the small cross which he made of wood and erected. Finally, reluctant to "remind the flesh of the dead of the deeds of a departed soul, faith and bedad," as he expressed it, he made the legend simply the name by which they had known the man. The name was:

BOB THOMAS